Mystery at Salt Marsh Bridge

Mystery at Salt Marsh Bridge

A Casey Miller Mystery

John M. Prophet

Writers Club Press
San Jose New York Lincoln Shanghai

Mystery at Salt Marsh Bridge
A Casey Miller Mystery

Writers Club Press
an imprint of iUniverse.com, Inc.

For information address:
iUniverse.com, Inc.
5220 S 16th, Ste. 200
Lincoln, NE 68512
www.iuniverse.com

ISBN: 0-595-17669-0

Printed in the United States of America

To my wife, Ellen, who waited patiently for the book to end.

Contents

Prologue

===

APRIL 10, 1898

*J*ason Pritchard was a proud man who hated surprises. He believed that his success was due to careful planning, rigid discipline and cultivation of a sterling reputation, although it could be argued that he failed miserably with the latter. In a few short hours he would get the surprise of his life and his whole life's work would be in jeopardy.

He paused for a moment on the steps of the state capitol. The smug look on his face showed the pleasure he felt at his latest accomplishment. This visit to the State House was particularly important. Jason was satisfied that, through his effort, he and his business partner, Oliver Colby, would achieve their goal of gaining political support for a vast land development project. His partner Oliver Colby usually handled this end of their business, but he had other commitments. Most of the time, Jason handled construction matters in the field and rarely found himself in front of groups where tact was needed to close a deal. Now, he felt that he could show Oliver that he could handle all sides of their business. Life, in general, couldn't be better.

Jason and Oliver were friends from early school days, but they decided to form their business partnership when they found themselves bidding on the same construction project. It was to the advantage of both to form a company and secure the contract as partners. Both found out early on that a merger of their individual talents would result in a powerful combination. That was fifteen years ago. Their instincts turned out to be true beyond their expectations. They achieved prosperity, power and the ability to shape the future of the whole South Coast area. After the partnership was formed, Oliver, a lawyer, handled the finer points of negotiating contracts and legal matters. He was a natural politician and he, too, believed in detailed planning. Jason, on the other hand, developed into an outspoken, bold, pompous and brassy job foreman, a stickler for details and rigid disciplinarian on the job. They were perfectly suited to each other. They were bold in their business dealings. They flaunted the law, flagrantly using bribes and favors in exchange for property rights and contracts. Even their acts of philanthropy, gifts to charity or donations of buildings, carried with them an air of opportunism. Nothing was ever given away without a promise of receiving more in return in the long run.

Jason glanced at ominous black clouds gathering in the southern sky, then looked up at the state capitol dome silhouetted against the darkening sky now bathed in the glow of sunset. Below him he could see Jeremiah Finch, an elderly stable hand, seated in the one-horse shay owned by Jason Pritchard and Oliver Colby. Jeremiah struggled with the reins to hold Baron, Jason's pride and joy, a high-spirited, ebony-black Arabian. The horse and carriage were a beautiful sight to behold. It was painted with shiny black enamel and decorated with swirls of gold leaf. Imprinted on the side in gold leaf was "Colby & Pritchard," a decorative advertisement for the partnership shared by the two men who dedicated their lives to accumulating wealth and political power. And Jason's personal appearance matched the splendor of the horse and carriage. He always dressed in a black, three-piece, specially tailored suit, with a stiffly-starched white shirt and a plain, a bright red tie. He never left his house without his shoes brightly shined.

Baron was more restless than usual. His hooves clattered on the cobblestone street as he struggled with Jeremiah.

"What's the matter, Jeremiah? Baron too much for you?" Jason's voice had a haughty air about it. He could not resist making fun of Jeremiah's struggles.

"Yes, sir, he's a fiery one. It took all I had to put the reins on him. I've handled many a horse for all you famous people, but none compare with Baron. There's a nor'easter blowin' in, Mr. Pritchard. You'll be gettin' high winds and high seas down your way. Baron may be just a mite touchy about the storm. Maybe you ought to stay the night."

Jason pulled on a gold chain attached to his vest. Out popped a gold, antique watch. He flipped open the cover and noted the time, 6:45 p.m.

"I'll be home by nine," said Jason. "No sense wasting money on a room for the night."

He did not enjoy leaving the city at this late hour. The idea of driving Baron through a storm made him nervous. However, Jason was a proud man. He would never shrink in the face of danger and his penny-pinching nature would not allow him the luxury of spending a night in an inn. The dirt roads and darkness always made it a treacherous journey even in the fairest weather. His home in Elm Grove by the Sea on the South Shore was thirty miles away.

Jason stepped up, adjusted his hulking, six foot two inch, two hundred and thirty-pound body and squeezed into the narrow seat beside Jeremiah. The one-horse shay creaked and sagged under his weight. Jason was a powerfully built man. Well fed would best describe him. His face was partially hidden behind a graying black beard and full mustache. He looked much older than his age, fifty-three. His beady, dark blue eyes, even when Jason was in fine spirits, gave him an air of sternness. His manner was tactless, coarse and gruff. His furrowed brow was a testimony to his lack of humor and constant state of agitation.

Jeremiah jumped out of the carriage and heaved a sigh of relief. Jason tossed a coin into the air and Jeremiah was there to catch it.

"I lit the lamps and put up the hood," said Jeremiah. "No question you'll be needin' 'em."

Jason nodded. The stately horse, carriage and driver headed south.

"Goodbye, sir. You have a safe trip." Jeremiah looked at the coin and muttered to himself. "He didn't even thank me. With all that trouble with that horse, I should have gotten twice this much."

Jason was an aggressive horseman. He loved giving Baron his head. Once clear of the city, Jason cracked his whip and Baron responded by galloping at great speed over the tree-lined dirt roads through Gatesville and Maplewood and southward to Elm Grove by the Sea. As the last glow of the setting sun disappeared, huge droplets of rain slapped noisily against the hood of the shay.

When Jason reached the border of Elm Grove, he could barely see through the rain blowing in sheets across his path. Deep pools of water formed on the muddy road. He was in the middle of a raging storm, racing through the darkness with thunder and lightning coming from all directions.

In Elm Grove, Ann Robertson waited for Hiram Kingsley to say a good-night to him at the Elm Grove Lending Library. She knew that Hiram looked forward to these brief moments. He always timed it perfectly. When she gathered up her belongings each night at closing time, she glanced toward the cellar door behind the checkout desk. The door would be slightly ajar and she knew that Hiram, a young man of thirty-five, but with the mental capacity of a ten-year-old, would emerge and march with her to the front entrance. He was in charge of locking up at 9:00 p.m. and relished his responsibility. Anne always befriended him and he was grateful to her for that.

"Goodnight, Hiram."

"Goodnight, Miss Robertson. You take care. It's rainin' awful hard."

Those were the last words they spoke to each other.

Through the blinding rain, Jason recognized a sign that read "Welcome to Elm Grove by the Sea." He pulled hard left on the reins, and Baron raced down Wood Road, the main thoroughfare to Elm Grove Harbor. Still cracking his whip, Jason urged Baron onward and turned right onto The Causeway, the only access road to Moss Island, a small strip of land off the coast of Elm Grove. He reached Salt Marsh Bridge, a structure that connected Moss Island, with the mainland. Suddenly, Baron shied.

"Whoa, Baron. What's the matter? Something on the road?"

Baron reared up on his hind legs and whinnied loudly. Jason pulled hard on the reins and shouted at him over the sounds of the wind and rain and, finally, Baron settled down. Jason took hold of a carriage lantern and dismounted making sure he held onto Baron's reins until he could fasten them to the fence that bordered The Causeway. There, at the side of the road was a body lying face down in the mud. Jason was stunned. He turned the body over. In the dim light of the lantern, he saw the side of a person's head, crushed. The rain washed the bloodied face.

"My god, it's a girl. It's Anne Robertson," he gasped. Nervously, he wiped the rain from his face, then felt the girl's neck to find a pulse. "She's dead. What am I going to do? The publicity will ruin us."

Jason trembled with fear. The friendly politicians he bargained with today would distance themselves from Colby and Pritchard like rats from a sinking ship and what would the community think?

"I have to talk with Oliver. He'll know what to do."

1

An Interesting Bit of News

Casey Miller slammed the door of the Principal's office. He had been sent there by a teacher with a note that read: For defiant behavior toward a teacher. The incident happened at the front entrance to the school. This was his second trip to the office, for the same thing. In the first visit he was given a warning, but this time his parents would be notified, but he didn't care. He felt lucky that he got no detention, but he still had to face his parents.

The heat in the hallway was stifling from the warmth of hundreds of bodies crowded together as relentless hot air poured from the wall vents of Elm Grove Junior High School. A musty odor from many damp winter jackets permeated the air. The rumbling sound of hundreds of students' footsteps on the wood hallway floor sounded like thunder. Locker doors slammed shut like a chorus of sledge hammers banging noisily on a tin roof and the sound of hundreds of jabbering teenagers was a continuous drone. It was an atmosphere that added fuel to Casey Miller's belligerence.

Casey paused for a moment at the top of a stairway leading to the school basement and looked down into the semi-darkness. A bead of perspiration dripped from his nose. He put his heavy book bag down, took off his faded blue baseball cap and wiped the perspiration from his forehead. He looked back at the hallway filled with the horde of students, scratched his head and made a halfhearted attempt to put his blond straggly hair back in place before he put his cap back on. As he bent down to pick up his school bag, the unruly mob in the hallway, moving like a tidal wave, bumped him. He had to grab a banister to keep from plummeting out of control down the stairs.

"Hey, watch out," he shouted at the mob. Casey was irritable today as he had been from the time he arrived in Elm Grove four months ago.

Casey was taller than most of his classmates, but thinly built. He certainly didn't weigh enough to withstand the onslaught of a herd of stampeding students. *Is this really a school?* It was not like this at his old school in Shorewood. The school principal would be out in the hallway screaming at the top of his lungs ordering everyone to line up and shut up, but not so at Elm Grove Junior High School.

He shrugged his shoulders and straightened his cap. At the bottom of the stairs, Casey found what he was looking for, the place where he could store his books and, finally, get rid of his ratty old book bag. Two tall, antique oak closets, feebly supported by four ungainly, lopsided legs, stood side by side, like wounded soldiers at attention. All that was missing was a bandage. It was Casey's bad luck to have moved to Elm Grove at a time when the school was overburdened with students and lockers scarce. He had to wait while whoever was in charge made a decision to move these monstrosities from the cellar of the abandoned Elm Grove Town Hall. At first glance, the two closets looked dilapidated, but they had withstood very well the test of time and were roomier than the ordinary hallway lockers. Best of all, their location out of the mainstream gave Casey the privacy he wanted. On one, one wooden leg was broken, probably by the men who lugged it in, causing the closet to tilt toward the wall. Neither one had a lock on it, but each one had a crude fastener artlessly attached to its door ready for a lock to satisfy a user's need for security. Though he hated to admit it, Casey was quite well satisfied with this arrangement.

"Well, first come, first serve," he muttered.

Casey took the closet closest to the stairs, despite its broken leg. He had waited for almost three months and he was tired of carrying everything he owned to all his classes in the silly looking book bag. The angry look on his face was not entirely due to the book bag. He had developed into an angry, bitter grouch and he didn't mind letting everyone in his path know it. It was against his better nature to be that way, but he had no interest in controlling it. If people knew what had happened in his life this past summer, maybe they would understand.

"It finally got here," he muttered aloud. "Now, I can burn this foolish book bag."

Casey reached inside the closet and rubbed his hand across a shelf and looked at the grimy, gray dust that stuck to his fingertips.

"What a mess!" Casey muttered, "No one even bothered cleaning this thing. What's this?"

It was a piece of paper, yellowed with age, stuck to the inside back wall. He picked up his notebook, opened it, and one small piece at a time, carefully removed and placed on a page what looked like an item from an old newspaper. With great difficulty, in the dim light, Casey read the faded print:

Memorial Service Held for Robertson Girl

Two hundred mourners attended a memorial service held yesterday afternoon at Elm Grove High School. A plaque was dedicated to the memory of Anne Robertson who disappeared without a trace.

The rest of the news item crumbled in his hand. Casey carefully closed his notebook with the remainder of the torn and tattered item inside. He thought about his best friend, Billy Keith, who died last August. *They sure aren't going to put up a plaque for Billy.*

A streak of sunlight broke through the overcast sky and, like a laser beam, came streaming through a window above the stairwell. Casey had to shade his eyes. When he looked into his locker, now clearly lit by the ray of light, he saw a small object wedged in between the base of the closet and the warped right side wall. Casey gave it a sharp tug and it came loose. It was a gold ring.

"I wonder how that got there," he thought.

Suddenly, the noise upstairs subsided. Apparently, the students were clearing the hallway. It was late. His first class was starting in less than five minutes. He put the ring in his pocket, stuffed his cap into the pocket of his jacket, took off his jacket and hung it on a hook in the back of the closet. Then he searched through his bag until he found the combination padlock he put there, pulled out the books for his first two classes and shoved the book bag onto the floor of the closet. He slammed the door, clipped on the padlock and turned to go upstairs. As he turned, he bumped into a girl.

"What's the rush?" the girl asked.

"I was just going to class," Casey replied. "That one's yours." He spoke with a gruff tone in his voice and pointed to the closet next to his.

"Thank you," she said, looking him straight in the eye. Her words lacked sincerity and her facial expression reflected a defensive temperament, obviously disturbed over his impoliteness.

Casey hesitated. He looked at the girl out of the corner of his eye. *I know this girl. We're in three classes together. I think her name is Alexandra or something like that.* She wore a tan ski jacket and tan corduroy slacks which made her look rather dull, but she couldn't hide an attractive, clear dark brown complexion, much like that of a good friend in Shorewood, Donny Nabors. Donny's family was the only black family in his neighborhood. Casey continued fumbling with his lock and watched as she took off her jacket, revealing a simple, freshly-starched white cotton blouse under a tan cardigan sweater. He stayed and, fiddling with his combination lock, pretended he needed something in his closet while keeping one eye on the girl. Something about her impressed him enough to remember her name. Their English teacher called on her a few times. She, too, had a school bag that she dropped to the floor. Hers was tan. When she took off a bright red knit cap, she ran both hands through her black, closely cut hair, then glanced at Casey. The frown on her face detracted from her pretty features.

"Can I help you with something?" she asked with the same defensiveness.

"No," replied Casey.

He continued to watch as Alexandra forced open her closet door and hung her jacket inside. She removed a notebook, textbook and a lock from her book bag and shoved the bag into the closet. After slamming the closet door and affixing a lock she looked Casey straight in the eye and walked by him without saying a word.

Casey followed her up the stairs. For some inexplicable reason, he wanted to get to know her. He had vowed not to get involved with people ever again, but it was harder than he expected. Four months of loneliness and frustration caught up with him. Alexandra reminded him of one of his friends in Shorewood. He missed his friends, a group of four boys and four girls who played together since they were three years old. Their "secret hangout" was The Sandbox at the neighborhood playground. There was more there than a sandbox for young children. There were picnic tables, too, covered with a roof held up by four large stanchions. It was a perfect meeting place, rain or shine. Over time, the site fell into disrepair. The mothers and fathers who once frequented the area with their children found other places for their children to play, so the town landscaping department stopped caring for the area. The group took over as unofficial owners of The Sandbox. Casey gave the group its name, The Sandbox Gang, when the members reached fifth grade.

Casey frequently recalled the events of the previous summer. In early August, his best friend, Billy Keith, along with his brother, Bobby and two friends, Rosie Germano and Donny Nabors, all members of The Sandbox Gang, broke into the Barker Lumber Yard in Shorewood. Billy died that night. Apparently he fell off the roof of one of the buildings. Bobby's anguished expression haunted Casey with mixed feelings of anger and sadness, because Bobby had put him in a precarious position.

Casey promised never to tell. When questioned by the police, Casey lied when he said he knew nothing about Billy's death. Later, he even lied to his parents, but he sensed that they knew he was lying. Within a few short weeks after that Casey moved to Elm Grove and the matter was never discussed again, but the matter had a profound effect on Casey.

Casey and his family just one week ago celebrated Thanksgiving with their usual feast of turkey and all the trimmings. It was not a happy Thanksgiving for Casey. He sat at the table slowly picking at his food. When offered a turkey drumstick, his favorite food, he refused and abruptly left the table when pressed by his family to explain the reason why. He spent the rest of the day in his room, gazing out his bedroom window at the restless ocean. When darkness closed in, he got into bed, curled up and went to sleep, not bothering changing into his pajamas. Sleep these days was a pleasant anesthetic.

When Casey reached the top of the stairs, Alexandra disappeared into a classroom. He would have given anything to have said something more to her, but he was too bottled up in his thoughts about last summer. *Why couldn't I say something to her? I hate it when I do that.* Thoughts came back to him about the news item he found in his closet, but more clearly the newspaper headlines about his friend Billy Keith: Teenager Killed After Break-in. It made Billy sound like a criminal. *They weren't going to put up any plaques for Billy.*

After school, Casey paused on the steps at the front entrance and watched a mass of students happily run to the yellow school buses lined up at the curbside. The buses belched white fumes into the cold clear New England air. Although the first snowfall had not arrived yet, Casey could feel the dampness in the air. Grayish clouds over head, saturated with moisture, obliterated the afternoon sun. From October to December the weather changes in this part of New England were dramatic. Nature, like a stage hand in a theater, decorated the stage in October with colorful Fall foliage. In November, Nature brought high winds and rain to strip the trees of foliage, thus, setting the stage for another change with the onslaught of bitter cold and snowy Winter storms.

Casey inhaled the crisp, cold air. It felt good after the stifling heat inside. He descended the stairs and paused in the driveway, took deep breaths to clear his lungs. He watched another line of buses move on between the two stone pillars marking the entrance to the school grounds. In one way, he wished he lived far enough away from school so he would be eligible to ride a bus. On the other hand, he was thankful that he could walk home by himself and wallow in his misery.

Casey spotted Alexandra. He watched her stop to look at a group of ten giggling girls waiting for a bus. All of them looked alike, dressed in blue and white plaid wool skirts with black tights, bundled up in colorful ski jackets with blue and white knit caps showing off the school colors. All but two had cheeks bulging with wads of gum which they busily worked on. In contrast, another group of girls at the same bus stop was dressed in oversized, baggy dungarees frayed at the bottoms. Some wore knit caps others were bareheaded. Three of these girls had wads of gum in their mouths evidenced by their working of their jaws. Two others, against school rules, had lit up cigarettes and were brazenly displaying them. A group of six boys, also clad in baggy, and beltless, dungarees which barely clung to slim hips, pranced around in macho fashion with their jackets open as if they were immune to the bitter cold. They were assembled close by nudging each other while they tossed comments back and forth at the girls. Alexandra, on the other hand, neat in appearance by comparison, wore her tan ski jacket. She wore tan mittens, faded tan corduroy pants and black walking shoes. Except for the red cap pulled down over her ears, she blended into the drab, colorless New England winter scenery. Her breath came out like puffs of smoke that quickly dissipated in the cold damp air. Over her shoulder she carried her out-of-date, tan book bag bulging with what looked like a heavy load. Without a word to the girls, and without a single glance at the boys, she continued her way off the school grounds. From Casey's vantage point, it looked like the girls intentionally avoided Alexandra, maybe because Alexandra was one of five black girls in school, maybe because they were just snobs who treated everyone that way. In any event, Casey felt drawn to Alexandra, because he, too, felt like an outsider.

A cold northeast wind whipped across Elm Grove Common carrying ice cold moisture from the Atlantic Ocean. It cut like a knife into Casey's face. He knew his nose would already be as red as Alexandra's cap. The first winter snow lurked in the clouds over head. It would, in all likelihood, snow during the night. Casey guessed the temperature was about his age, fifteen. His jacket protected his chest but his knees, covered only with a light pair of jeans, felt like they had ice packs wrapped around them.

On an impulse, Casey ran after Alexandra and shouted. "Alexandra! Alexandra, wait a minute."

"Are you talking to me?" she asked curtly.

"Yeah, can you hold up for a minute?"

"What do you want?" Her face showed annoyance at his approach.

"I just want to show you something I found in my locker, that's all."

Casey shielded his notebook from the wind and showed her his discovery.

"It's only a piece of an old newspaper clipping. What's the big deal?"

"Read what it says."

She quickly scanned the item. "So?"

"What do you think?" *This was really a stupid thing to do. How can I tell her I just wanted to talk to her?*

"Why are you asking me? Why don't you ask one of those girls back there?" Her voice was sarcastic in its tone and Casey thought it was a bit snobbish.

"Hey, forget it." Casey started to get angry and frustrated with himself for putting himself in a situation he wasn't prepared to handle. He turned to walk away.

Alexandra's voice softened. "Wait. I'm sorry. I'm not used to talking with people here."

"I don't know anyone else, either," said Casey. "You're the first person I've said more than two words to since I moved here." This time his tone of voice was more conciliatory.

"Don't you hang out with any of the guys?" Alexandra's voice softened, too.

"No. They probably wouldn't be interested in this anyway."

"What makes you think I'm interested?"

"I don't know. I took a chance. You could just as easily have found this, only I took the first closet. Look, just forget the whole thing."

"But, I might not have asked you about it. I don't know anyone either. People aren't exactly falling over themselves to meet me. Why are you so interested in this girl?"

Casey avoided the question. "Can I walk with you?"

"Sure, why not, but only if you call me Lexie." Casey thought he detected a slight smile.

"Your book bag looks heavy. You could have left some of the books in school. Let me carry it."

"Why? Don't you think I'm strong enough?"

"I didn't mean it that way. I just thought I could help."

"Sorry. I didn't mean to bite your head off. Thanks for asking."

"Let's trade. You carry mine and I'll carry yours."

"That's a great idea."

Since moving to Elm Grove, Casey had avoided contact with people. He hated moving to this small seacoast town, but it really wasn't Elm Grove he hated, it was the move away from The Sandbox Gang. The timing of the move to Elm Grove was terrible, but he realized that it had nothing to do with Billy Keith's death. The fact that his father took an opportunity he couldn't turn down just happened to coincide with the untimely death of his best friend. He was all mixed up, filled with guilt, mourning the loss of his friend, frustrated over the promise he made to Bobby, and depressed over his having to move away from The Sandbox. Now, for whatever reason, he reached out to Lexie and it felt good.

Casey jammed his notebook into his book bag and gave it to Lexie and, in turn, took hers. Jokingly, he let her bag flop to the ground.

"Whoa, what's here, a bowling ball?"

"If you're not strong enough…" Again, Casey detected a slight smile.

Casey grinned. "I think I can handle it."

He stuffed his left hand into his jacket pocket. Out of the corner of his eye, he looked to see how much taller he was. He was relieved to see that he was at least three inches taller and he straightened his back to appear even taller. Together they went down Old Country Lane, the main thoroughfare extending from the state highway through a residential area of historic homes into Elm Grove Harbor.

"My name is Casey Miller."

"I know. Mine's Lexie Wentworth. I just moved into town last summer."

She knows my name. "I moved here around the same time you did, from the North Shore, Shorewood. Where did you come from?"

"San Francisco."

"The only place I've been is New Hampshire. I've heard a lot of strange stories about San Francisco."

"It's not so strange, just a lot of different people doing their own thing."

"Did you live in the city?"

"Yes, we had a condominium overlooking San Francisco Bay."

"That sounds really good. Why did you move?"

"My father works for IBM and he got a big promotion, so he had to move. That's the way it goes in his business. This is our third move. We hope it's the last. Have you heard of army brats? You know, kids who move a lot? Well, I'm an IBM brat."

"So I noticed," said Casey with a grin.

"I'm sorry I snapped at you."

"Any brothers or sisters?"

"No."

"I still haven't made up my mind about our move. My father picked up a good deal on a fishing boat here and we stumbled onto the house we live in, so it's a good move for my parents. They both graduated from Elm Grove High."

"This is just another new adventure for me. I'm used to the changes. We thought my mother might mind it a lot. She's a Californian, but she likes this place a lot. She works out of our house as an illustrator for a book publisher, so she didn't have to make a job change."

"She's an artist?"

"A good one. Art is my favorite subject, too. I'd like to do what she's doing some day, but I don't think I'm talented like she is. My father graduated from Elm Grove High, too, so he was really happy to come back."

"Don't you have a lot of friends here?" Casey wished he could take that question back. He knew all too well that Black students, any new-comers for that matter, were treated coolly in Elm Grove Junior High.

"No, but I'll be all right. All the girls seem to be in tight little groups here. I don't fit in with any of them. It wasn't like that in San Francisco. You're not in any groups either."

"My sister is doing a lot better at it than me. Kathy's the type who just fits in everywhere. I hardly see her at all anymore. She's sixteen, goes to the high school. My mother and father went steady in high school and were married here, so they know the town pretty well."

"You're not so bad after all," said Lexie.

"What do you mean?"

"I hear things."

"What things?"

"You know. Kids talk."

"Talk about what?"

"Well, they think you're kind of weird, I guess, always mad. Are you?"

"I guess I have been a little cranky. I've got a few things on my mind."

"Hey, if you want to talk about it sometime…"

"Do you have a bike?"

"Yes. Why?"

Lexie was taken aback by the quick change in the conversation.

"The news clip says there's a plaque at the high school. You know, for Anne Robertson? I have to go to the library and I thought I'd go see it before the high school closes. Would you like to go?" Casey held his breath. *She would surely say no.*

"I'd like that." And Casey saw that slight smile, again.

There was a lull in the conversation for a moment, then Lexie asked a question that seemed to come out of nowhere.

"Do you smoke?" she asked.

"No, do you?"

"No."

Each appeared satisfied with the other's answer. They continued without another word.

They came to the end of Old Country Lane. It ended at the intersection of three roads called Pritchard's Corner, marked by a statue of Jason Pritchard dedicated to honor his contributions to Elm Grove more than one hundred years ago. Across the street from the statue was a vacant lot where the town put up and decorated a tall Christmas tree with colorful strings of lights. The lights would come on by timer at five-thirty every day until New Year's Day. One of the roads, to the North, was Harbor Avenue, now decorated with many lines of white Christmas lights hung across the street from building to building. This was the primary shopping area of Elm Grove. In the opposite direction, Wood Road wound its way southward along the coast and joined the state highway at the south end of Elm Grove. And the other, The Causeway, ran easterly over Salt Marsh Bridge, the only access road to the Colby Shore area where Casey and Lexie lived. The bridge spanned a narrow tidal stream connecting Elm Grove Harbor to the North with a salt marsh bordering Wood Road to the South. At the bridge, east of the tidal stream, The Causeway turned left and continued northward along Colby Shore, ending at the Elm Grove Coast Guard Station. Sandy Point Lane branched off The Causeway at the bridge and ran southward to Lexie's house and a quarter of a mile further to a high promontory known as Sandy Point.

As Casey and Lexie crossed Salt Marsh Bridge, a gust of ice cold wind almost stopped them in their tracks. The temperature was typical of New England in early December. It would drop to the single digits by nightfall. The wind in their faces made the temperature feel like below zero degrees. The salt marsh had started to freeze. In a few short weeks, only the tops of the marsh grass would be seen sticking up through the ice.

"Do you still want to go for the ride?" asked Casey, "It's really cold," he added, shivering as he spoke. "We can go another time."

"I won't mind if you don't."

"I'll meet you at the bridge in twenty minutes." They swapped book bags and waved goodbye.

As Casey walked along The Causeway, he was amazed at how desolate the area looked. At this time of year, at least during the week, there wasn't a sign of life. On his left, Bradley's Boat Yard, bustling with activity in the summertime, was now as quiet as a graveyard crowded with the hulks of hundreds of boats stored for the winter. A few diehards spent weekends working on their boats, but, for the most part, by December, this part of Elm Grove was a deserted, forgotten stretch of land. On his right was a row of four beach houses now boarded up for the winter. Each house was built facing the boat yard to the West and the Atlantic Ocean to the East. Except for a small paved parking area in the front of each house, all the houses were surrounded by beach sand speckled with clumps of coarse, reedy grass. Casey's house, was on the approved list of historic homes, having been built in 1894. For more than a hundred years it withstood the heavy winds and pounding waves driven by Northeast storms which frequented this part of the country, especially in the Fall and Winter. The Causeway continued to the top of Admiral's Point to the Coast Guard Station lookout tower and barracks. Casey's house was the last house on the street, situated about one hundred yards from the entrance to the Coast Guard Station. It was an oversized Cape Cod style house sided with dark gray, weathered shingles and bordered with white trim.

Over Bradley's Boat Yard Casey saw the sky glowing with a soft mixture of colors, orange, red and purple. In a little more than two hours the sun would set. Already it felt colder as Casey walked into the lengthening shadows from the boatyard. He shivered as the damp ocean breeze quickened. The space between the beach houses formed a wind tunnel. He had to hold onto his cap when a gust of turbulent wind came up unexpectedly.

The cellar entrance to Casey's house was a bulkhead close to the street. He lifted one of two doors covering a stairwell, took two steps down to the main cellar door and made his way through a maze of boxes not yet unpacked since his family moved in. His bicycle leaned against the wall near the door. Tools and equipment of a commercial fisherman were everywhere. Nets dangled from the ceiling, white and red striped buoys stood neatly arranged against one wall. Two small anchors peeked out from behind a sheet of canvas. Spools of fishing line, tool boxes, and assorted fishing gear cluttered a makeshift tool bench. The cellar walls, made from fieldstone, were patched with dark gray cement to keep moisture out.

Casey ran up the cellar stairs. He shivered as the warm air from the kitchen engulfed him. Despite the harsh winds sweeping in from the Atlantic Ocean, the house was very warm. No one was at home. His father would be at the dock in Elm Grove Harbor preparing for his next fishing trip, probably the last of the year. His mother would be at Dr. Ames' office. Kathy, Casey's sister, would, most likely, be at the Harbor Mall with her friends. Casey dropped his book bag by the kitchen door, went into the dining room and plugged in two sets of white, Christmas candle lights in the front and side windows, returned to the kitchen and plugged in two there. It would be another two weeks before the family put up its Christmas tree. Casey walked through the living room and stepped outside onto a wide deck overlooking the ocean.

Since moving to Elm Grove, Casey had developed a daily routine of looking at what was happening on the beach. A gust of wind nearly blew his cap off. He looked eastward at the whitecaps dotting the ocean's surface made frothy by the strong northeast breeze. He spread his arms and took a deep breath to suck in the clean salt air. This is what Casey loved most about Elm Grove. His old house in Shorewood was much smaller and on a crowded side street with no view of the ocean.

When he was not walking alone on the beach, Casey was alone in his room, staring out his bedroom window or shutting out the world with music blaring through the earphones of his Walkman radio. At other times he might spend time in the cellar repairing small pieces of equipment for his father. Casey was good with his hands and he enjoyed the feeling of accomplishment when he got something to work. He needed this activity to anesthetize him from the pain he was feeling about Billy Keith's death and everything connected with it. He liked to compare himself to his father, a man who spent days at sea with only one other person to help him on his boat. His father was a quiet man totally committed to making his living from the sea, independent and solid as a rock. But, Casey was sensitive and emotional, too, much like his mother. He longed for the same peace of mind his father seemed to have, but he wasn't clear on how to get there. It took only one fishing trip with his father to convince him that he would not pursue the life of a fisherman. He was content some days, but there were days when he would run on the beach to a point of exhaustion trying to burn off his frustration. No matter how hard he tried he could not outrun his worries. They held on as tight as his shadow.

"Looks like a storm is coming."

He often talked aloud to himself when he was alone. There were times, as he walked alone on the beach, when he would turn into the wind and scream the first word that entered his mind. It relieved some of his frustration. A fleeting thought about the death of his friend entered his mind, but he quickly turned his attention to the vast expanse of ocean. Casey's attention was drawn to a wandering seagull soaring over head. He watched with interest as the graceful bird dove for a clam shell, pecked at it and then picked it up and flew off. That's the way it was with Casey. Sometimes the whole story of that fateful night and the following days would come rushing back, clear and chilling. At other times, like now, he would only think of fragments that he could easily set aside, especially when he allowed himself to relax. He thought about Ann Robertson and wondered why no one ever found her.

After taking another deep breath to inhale more of the salt air, Casey returned to the kitchen, poured himself a glass of milk and slapped some peanut butter between two slices of bread. He carried his feast to the cellar, took one big gulp of milk and left the glass on the tool bench. With his mouth filled with peanut butter and bread and milk he maneuvered his bicycle through the bulkhead door and into the street. Lexie was waiting for him at Salt Marsh Bridge. For the first time in a very long time, he was excited about meeting someone.

"Hi," said Casey.

"Hi."

That was the extent of their conversation until they got to Elm Grove High School. Only a few cars remained in the parking lot and a few stragglers met them at the front door.

"It must be in the lobby somewhere," said Casey. He led the way in.

Directly ahead, they spotted a large trophy case filled with statuettes and plaques representing championships won by the Elm Grove High School sports teams. More plaques of different sizes and shapes lined the wall beside it.

"There it is," said Lexie.

A round wooden plaque, with a dark aged brass plate, was engraved with:

'IN MEMORIAM, Ann Robertson, 1871-1898.'

"Can you believe that?" asked Casey. "The article I found must have been written in 1898."

"What do we do now?"

"Library, I guess."

2

A Visit to the Library

"I don't know what it is about this place, but it gives me the creeps," said Lexie.

"Me, too."

Leafless trees cast eerie, flickering shadows across the front of the Elm Grove Town Library. The brittle branches of stately oak and elm trees rattled against the windows. The tips of their branches, which long ago should have been trimmed away, crackled against each other and scratched at the building with annoying persistence. These trees were donated as seedlings by some well-meaning Elm Grove townspeople when the library was built in 1898. The donors could not have foreseen the damage they would cause. Nor could they have foreseen that citizens' groups in modern day would debate long and hard with each other trying to decide whether or not the trees should be cut down, trimmed properly or remain untouched. So far, the remain-untouched crowd was winning for it was easier to table the matter rather than risk an unpopular vote. Since the very existence of the building was in question, it would be better not to allocate funds for the trees until a vote was taken on the disposition of the library. Now, the mature trees with massive trunks and broad-reaching branches pushed and shoved to make room for each other. Underground the enormous roots burrowed their way into the building foundation, threatening the underpinnings of a once-elegant structure. In Spring and summer, the trees provided shade and kept the building cool. In the Fall, they covered the building with colorful leaves of golden yellow, fiery red, and bright orange. On this cold December day, they stood like huge dark brown skeletons fighting against a stiff, offshore breeze, punishing the building with their incessant scrapings.

Although it was still about two hours before sunset, the overcast sky and dense shrubbery darkened the entire front of the library. The windows glowed like cat eyes peering out of the darkness One string of multicolored-lights outlined the top of the building in a half-hearted attempt to make a showing for the Christmas holiday season.

Wide granite steps led to a front porch where four tall, fluted pillars guarded the main entrance. Two black, wrought-iron lamps glowed, with an eerie soft light, one on each side of the front door. Next to the front entrance a bronze plaque, blackened with age and weather, commemorated the original Elm Grove Library Association founders: Oliver L. Colby, Chairman, Jason M. Pritchard, Henry G. Stoneham, Stanley K. Morris, and James L. Samuelson.

Elm Grove was a quiet coastal village with a rich heritage dating back to the early settlers in the sixteen hundreds. Virtually every street had at least one historical landmark. Elm Grove, like most growing towns, had its share of developments. It was common to see a modern split-level house next to a two-hundred-year-old Cape style house, the former occupied by a computer expert from the West coast, the latter occupied by the descendants of the earliest settlers. The old folkways of the town were being challenged by newcomers who wanted the town to progress. The library was one of the focal points of that challenge.

Casey and Lexie entered the building through a heavy oak door adorned with images of Santa Claus' head stuck to each of two smoked glass windows. A small anteroom protected the main reading area from the cold. Casey pushed open an inner swinging door and held it open as

Lexie passed through.

A group called Citizens for the Preservation of Historic Buildings claimed, though it was never proved, that the partnership of Oliver Colby and Jason Pritchard had found the building plans of Thomas Jefferson's home and used them, with a few alterations, to build the library. That group wanted to keep the building intact, but many changes had been made to fit a variety of needs. It was the growth of the town and the explosion of information that forced a helter-skelter modernization of the building despite persistent outcries. All of the original rooms were furnished with overstuffed sofas and chairs accompanied by rich mahogany tables with elegant floor lamps to light the reading area, all arranged to provide wealthy patrons with maximum privacy. But, under increasing demand, large study tables with individual study lamps replaced the stuffed sofas and chairs. Space in a rear entryway was used to house a small elevator for the disabled. Carrels for listening to tapes and records were installed along the west wall at the expense of shelving. Makeshift rooms were constructed by positioning dividers to handle children's programs and additional demands for business materials.

The Elm Grove Historical Society, under pressure from a group of citizens, reluctantly agreed to preserve one of the rooms next to the main room and named it the Colby-Pritchard Reading Room. It was roped off to preserve it as it was before the building was turned over to the town in the mid 1930's to be managed by the Historical Society. A bitter dispute arose because the Historical Society had no interest in dignifying Colby and Pritchard, but, other groups in the town felt that, like it or not, Colby and Pritchard were part of Elm Grove's rich history. They kept the same oriental carpet and two faded, high-back stuffed chairs, one once belonging to Oliver Colby and the other from the estate of Jason Pritchard. Each chair was flanked by Victorian style end tables arranged in front of a fieldstone fireplace tall enough for Casey to stand up in. There were three fireplaces in the building. In the early days, the fireplaces provided the only heat for the building during the cold months. For building codes and safety reasons the fireplaces had not been used for many years. Two large paintings were hung on each side of the fireplace, one of Oliver Colby, on the left and the other of Jason Pritchard on the right. They were lit with small brass lamps one above each painting accentuating the regal elegance of the two founders and builders of the Elm Grove Library,

Several paintings of other prominent citizens of the town dating back many years hung in small alcoves on each wall in the main room. Rich-looking, cherry-wood paneling covered the walls. The uncarpeted dark-stained oak floor, despite the wear from years of traffic was as shiny as a bowling alley.

In the main room an undignified rubber mat paved the way directly from the front door to the main checkout desk. Shelves, packed with books, lined the walls using every inch of space. Two balconies, now decorated with plastic ivy and lines of tiny white Christmas lights, stretched from front to back, accessible by way of the elevator for the disabled and two stairways located in each rear corner. The most impressive object, dominating the center of the domed ceiling in the main room, was a large chandelier glistening with imported crystal ornaments.

Every year, for the past five years, proposals for a modern structure were presented to the Town meetings, but no agreement could be reached on what to do with this decaying, but still elegant building. Apparently, the two men who donated the property and building, Oliver Colby and Jason Pritchard were more concerned about building a monument to themselves than they were about providing a place where the public could browse. Originally, it was built for exclusive use of the wealthy, not as a public library, but as a place to meet in a quiet, elegant setting undisturbed by the masses. It was Oliver Colby's idea and Jason Pritchard handled the construction. Now, an outdated heating system was losing its battle with the cold drafts of air leaking through ancient cracks and crevices. No amount of elegance could prevent the settling of the building and a constant invasion of dampness from the earthen crawl space below. Sooner or later, the building would have to be replaced or undergo expensive major renovations.

Despite its ponderous appearance and its cramped space, the library attracted large numbers of people, but this afternoon traffic was relatively light. The cold weather undoubtedly had an effect and it was close to dinnertime. Casey and Lexie found an empty table near the checkout counter.

"I have to look up something for History class, about the Town Meetings. What are you going to do?" asked Lexie.

"I have a book report to do. I haven't made up my mind yet."

"Why don't you try a mystery story? Maybe there's one about Anne Robertson."

Her voice had a mild touch of sarcasm, but Lexie ended the sentence with a grin.

"I like mysteries. Maybe I'll look for one." Casey, again, avoided Lexie's attempt to get him to talk about why he was so interested in Anne Robertson. He browsed through the mystery section, chose a book by Erle Stanley Gardner and returned to the table.

"I'll be finished in a minute," said Lexie.

"Take your time. I'm in no hurry."

Casey really wasn't in a hurry. As far as he was concerned, this date with Lexie could go on for hours. He sat across the table from her and watched as she busily made notes from an old book. He fidgeted in his seat looking for something to do and recalled the plaque at the high school. The words In Memoriam played over and over in his mind, like a song that sticks in one's head. And then, he remembered the ring. He took it from his pocket and just as he was about to examine it, Lexie interrupted him.

"I'm done," she whispered. "What have you got there?"

"I was just thinking about the plaque and then I remembered I found this ring in my closet, too. Here, take a look."

"There's an inscription on the inside. It says, JP to AR '98."

Casey took the ring back.

"This is a real antique. Could the AR be Anne Robertson?"

"Then who would JP be?"

"Now I've got you thinking about it. Do you think they'd have some copies of old yearbooks here?"

"Let's ask the librarian. There she is at the desk."

"What'll I say? I feel kind of foolish asking for a one-hundred-year-old yearbook."

"Do you want me to do it?" asked Lexie with a shy grin.

"No, I can do it."

Dorothy Moorehead, Head Librarian, stood behind an ornately carved checkout counter busily applying a handkerchief to her nose, nursing a sinus condition that plagued her for all five years of her library service. She was only the fourth Director, hired since the private library was turned over to the Town in 1935, a span of sixty-five years. There was something bland and emotionless in the way Dorothy related to people and this was annoying to most borrowers, but, she was competent in her job and that was sufficient. Her private lifestyle was extravagant and did not go unnoticed by the town gossip-mongers. Casey's mother worked for Doctor Ames, Elm Grove's most popular doctor. She had already picked up that much from Dr. Ames' patients and shared it with Casey's family at the supper table. The salary Dorothy received as Library Director, according to the gossip, was certainly not enough to support her obvious extravagance. She dressed well in current fashions, had a standing weekly appointment with the local hairdresser and manicurist, drove a late model car and kept her modest home meticulously neat and well landscaped. On her vacations she traveled to exotic places, obviously, very expensive. Her husband died shortly after they arrived in Elm Grove, so it was assumed that her apparent wealth came from insurance money. Her husband was unemployed during a long illness before he died. Where else, after all, could the wealth come from?

"Excuse me," he whispered. "Could you help us?"

"Yes, what is it?" Dorothy asked through her handkerchief. Her muffled voice did not hide her condescending tone.

She retrieved her horn-rimmed glasses from her dark brown hair, neatly curled in a stylish hairdo. She placed them on the bridge of her finely-sculptured nose now reddened from the frequent use of her handkerchief. Most people considered Dorothy an attractive woman. From a distance, she looked much younger than her forty-odd years. Up close, Casey noticed the faint line of a scar under her right eye. Her oval face, with beady eyes accented by high cheekbones, thin lips, and a narrow, sculptured nose, showed signs of wrinkles across her forehead. She was slightly taller than Casey, but her erect posture made her seem taller. A black cardigan sweater gave her the extra warmth the heating system could not provide. A pair of stylish, black, laced high top boots disappeared under a full-length paisley skirt. She dressed and acted as if she was the lady of a manor, usually in long skirts to hide her bony figure. Casey felt a chill go up his spine. He couldn't tell if it was caused by a cold draft or from Dorothy's piercing stare.

"We're looking for the old Elm Grove High School yearbooks. Do you have any?" Casey asked. He caught himself, glanced at Lexie, and, for some reason he himself could not understand, avoided saying 1898.

"All of the yearbooks are in the cellar. We're very lucky to have them. Our oldest books were donated by a woman's group. We don't get many calls for them. Is this for a school project?"

Neither Casey nor Lexie expected the question, so they stood silently for a moment, not knowing how to reply.

"No, ma'am. We're just curious," said Lexie.

Casey showed his satisfaction with Lexie's reply by tapping her gently on her back. Tacitly, both understood that it would be better to forego explaining in detail what they were looking for. They would not want to risk an unwanted debate over their reason, especially with the likes of Dorothy Moorehead.

Dorothy Moorehead opened a door behind her, flipped a switch and led the way down a steep staircase into a dimly lit cellar.

"There isn't much light down here, so watch your step," Dorothy warned.

At the bottom of the stairs, they stepped onto a concrete floor where several rows of metal prefabricated shelves stood in tight rows. It was a dimly-lit room with a ceiling and walls of unfinished plaster board. The original structure had no cellar, just a dirt crawl space. In the past year, volunteers dug out half of that crawl space and poured a cement floor to make a storage area. An electric space heater glowed in one corner heating the cellar area, a feeble attempt at keeping the area dry to preserve the materials until a more permanent solution could be funded. It was the cheapest way the library could gain more space for storage. The plan for the future was to expand the existing floor and build a well-insulated storage area for the town archives.

Dorothy pointed to the far side of the room and said, "If you will move those boxes, you will see the old yearbooks on the bookshelf. I'll be upstairs if you need me." Loudly, she blew her nose and ascended the stairs.

A single light bulb dangled from the center of the room casting eerie shadows as it swayed in the breeze created by Casey and Lexie passing it. Casey took hold of it and pointed it toward the unfinished section of the crawl space where mounds of dirt were held back by a cement block retaining wall. A makeshift curtain was installed to cover the unfinished area, but part of it hung loose to expose what was there.

"It's really creepy down here. Let's find the book and get out of here," said Lexie.

There were three shelves filled with yearbooks all in order by year. Casey and Lexie could see that the older volumes were much thinner and in very poor condition. Carefully, Lexie pulled out one of the faded books. It was the one from 1905. To the left she found the one dated 1898. It was not exactly a yearbook by modern standards. Its cover was made of heavy dull gray paper. The title across the middle, Seascape was in faded black letters and below that, the year1898 appeared, also faded.

They returned to the main library and took seats in a far corner away from the main desk. Lexie opened the yearbook. The pages were stiff and stuck together. She carefully turned the pages, anxiously looking for a picture of Anne Robertson. The yearbook did not have the flair and organization of a current yearbook. Photographs were dim and the poses of the class members were stiff and formal. It may have been the first publication of a yearbook for Elm Grove High School.

"They look like they weren't too happy about getting their picture taken," said Casey.

"There she is." Lexie pressed closer to Casey.

Anne's picture appeared on a separate page. The words In Memoriam were inscribed above it and below, 1871 - 1898.

For a moment Casey and Lexie sat silently staring at Anne Robertson. Unlike her classmates, Anne was smiling broadly and her short, cropped hair gave her a boyish look. There was something impish in the way she smiled. Apparently, it was a photograph from home instead of the formal yearbook picture.

Casey finally broke the silence.

"The news item said she disappeared without a trace. She was just two years older than we are when she disappeared. What do you think happened to her?"

Lexie turned back a few pages until she came to the group of students whose last names began with the letter P. Only one student's name, Jonathan Pritchard, had both letters that appeared on the ring. Unlike Anne's, his picture showed Jonathan with a profoundly dejected look on his face.

"He looks a little like you," whispered Lexie. She grinned as she poked him with her elbow.

"Here's the real clue. Look what's written next to his picture."

"Anne will be missed. That's all there is. No listing of clubs or awards or anything," said Lexie.

"It's time to go home. It's getting late." Casey spoke abruptly and it startled Lexie.

Casey closed the yearbook and dropped it into the book return slot at Dorothy Moorehead's desk and without another word headed for the front door. Neither Casey nor Lexie noticed that Jake Colby, the library custodian, took the yearbook out of the book return and glared at them as they left.

Lexie followed Casey down the steps and as they mounted their bicycles, Lexie said, "Was it something I said? I really don't think you look like Jonathan."

"It's not you," said Casey. As he spoke, he rode away from Lexie and headed toward Salt Marsh Bridge.

Lexie rode behind Casey, muttering, "It's not me? It's not me? Is that all there is? He's got me talking to myself."

Casey stopped at Salt Marsh Bridge and waited for Lexie. As she approached, she looked straight ahead and was about to ride by Casey.

"Wait," said Casey. "I'm sorry."

"You don't have to be sorry about anything. I just don't know what to do when you walk away from me like I didn't exist. What do you mean, it's not me?" Lexie's tone of voice was harsher than she really wanted it to be and she wished that she could start over.

"I don't blame you for wondering what's going on. I just can't talk about it, that's all."

"Well, that's a better answer than before."

"Want to walk to school together tomorrow."

"Sure."

"OK, see you then."

Casey rode off toward home. Lexie paused for a moment to watch him, then slowly pushed her bicycle up Sandy Point Road more confused than ever.

*   *   *

At supper that evening, Casey sat quietly, poking at the food on his plate thinking about his day at school, especially about the principal calling his parents, afterward at the library, and Lexie's phone call. Casey's father was still at the dock working on his boat. His mother and his sister, Kathy, were eating and chatting with each other as if he wasn't there. They always ate in the early evening because of the different schedules.

"What happened at school today?" asked Casey's mother.

"Nothing," replied Casey. His head was bowed and he mumbled when he spoke.

"Nothing? Mr. Williams told me something else."

"What did he say?"

"He said that you were rude to a teacher and that you refused to answer him when he asked you a question."

"It was none of his business."

"None of his business? The teacher must have had a good reason to ask you something."

"He thought I was at the wrong door. He asked to see my schedule."

"Well?"

"Well, what?"

"Did you show him?"

"What for? I was at the right door."

"Then what?"

"I told him I was at the right door and walked away."

"When did Mr. Williams get involved?"

"He caught me in the hall."

"Did you answer him back, too?"

"No."

"Mr. Williams told me he let you off with just a warning. He said this was your second time in the office. Next time he won't be so lenient."

"Three strikes and you're out," interjected Kathy.

"Never mind, Kathy."

"I'll talk to your father when he gets home."

Casey slumped in his chair. The last thing he wanted to do was to disappoint his parents. His mother and Kathy resumed eating.

"I bought a ring today," said Casey's mother. She opened a small box.

"Let me see," said Kathy. "It looks like an old Elm Grove High class ring."

"It is. I bought it at the Elk's Christmas Craft Fair. I never had a class ring and couldn't help buying it."

"You and Dad graduated together, right?" asked Kathy.

"Right. We were high school sweethearts. We were together so often, the other kids called us Mr. and Mrs."

"What did you do after graduation?"

"That was in 1964. We got married right after graduation and your father took a job in Shorewood on a commercial fishing boat. The Vietnam War was going strong and, in 1966, your father was drafted into the Army and he spent two years in Vietnam. I got a job as a receptionist in Shorewood and just waited for him to come home."

"You must have been happy to see him."

"I was. We had never been apart for that long and I hope it never happens again."

Casey kept picking at his food, ignoring their conversation.

"When your father returned from Vietnam in 1968, he went back to work with the same fishing company. We saved every penny we could. Your father wanted his own boat very badly. It was just this past summer that he got a chance to buy a fishing boat from an old friend. And so, we moved back to Elm Grove. The timing wasn't exactly perfect for you and Casey but if he didn't act, he would have missed what he thought was a once-in-a-lifetime opportunity."

"I don't mind. Really, I don't. I felt bad at first, but I'm getting along fine in school. But, Casey isn't. What about you, Casey?"

Dan ignored her.

"How did we get this great house, Mom?" asked Kathy.

"We came down here before we moved to look for a place and found out that the Elm Grove Historical Society was looking for someone to buy this house. Over the years, the house had maintenance problems, and they had trouble raising money to keep the place. The house had a bad reputation. Historians weren't too kind to Oliver Colby and the townspeople were not too enthusiastic about supporting this project. It seems that Oliver was a greedy man. He and his partner, Jason Pritchard, destroyed important landmarks and upset the environment and scenery of the town with expansions of housing developments. He put a whole bunch of people out of work when he built this house. The Society would rather have had the Colby house torn down, but that, too, was an expensive proposition. It was a better idea to sell the house and recover some funds than leave an empty, unproductive lot on the beach. We just happened to be here at the right time, met with the President of the society, made an offer and it was accepted. Not only that, the Historical Society willingly helped secure the mortgage for us."

"This is a great house. I love the ocean," said Kathy. "Don't you, Casey?"

Again, Casey ignored her.

"Boy, the kids at school are right. What a grouch."

"He's just got a lot on his mind," said Mrs. Miller.

"Is the ring a present for someone —- like me?" asked Kathy.

"No, it's for me. When your father and I graduated from high school, neither of our families could afford to buy us a class ring. Your father and I wanted one, very badly. I guess everyone got one, except us. I never thought about it until I saw this one. It isn't exactly like the one we would have had in 1964, but it will do. See? It has Elm Grove HS around the stone. And there, '98 is above it. I'm going to take it to a jeweler to have the number changed to '64. And, I'm going to have the inscription changed and give it to your father so we can go steady."

Kathy chuckled, then congratulated her on her find. Casey was lost in his thoughts.

Kathy reached over and poked Casey. "Hear that, Casey? Mom and Dad might even get married."

Casey grunted.

"What's the matter with you? You've been a grouch since we moved here."

"Leave me alone, Kathy," said Casey.

"You weren't like that last year. Was it something I said?"

"For the last time, leave me alone."

"All the kids at school call him The Grinch. If we're not careful, Casey might steal Christmas. Casey was a good kid last year. What happened?"

Casey picked up his plate, put it in the sink and started to go to his room. He was angry about everything. There was nothing his family, or anyone else for that matter, could do to make Casey happy.

"What does the inscription say?" Kathy asked her mother.

"It says AR to JMP, 3/98," said Julie.

Casey almost jumped out of his skin. "What?" he cried, "What did you say? Can I see it?" He took the ring. "It couldn't be," he mumbled.

"What did you say?" asked Julie.

"Mom, what's the matter with Casey?" asked Kathy.

"Nothing's the matter with me."

He threw the ring onto the table and raced to the telephone. He had to tell Lexie. Two rings in one day both with Anne Robertson inscriptions. How could that be possible? Casey's fingers raced over the buttons on the phone.

"Hello, can I speak with Lexie, please? This is Casey Miller."

"I'm Lexie's mother. Lexie told us about you. I think your father and Mr. Wentworth went to school together. Hold on a minute."

Casey tapped his foot, scratched his head, stared at the ceiling and was about to hang up when he heard Lexie speak.

"Hello?" Lexie asked.

"It's me. Casey Miller."

"Hi, Casey."

"You aren't going to believe this. My mother bought an old Elm Grove High School class ring today. It says 'AR to JMP, 3/98' on it. What do you think of that? The year has to be 1898 and AR has to be Anne Robertson."

"That's really strange."

"We're walking to school together tomorrow, right?"

"Yes. I'll see you at the bridge? I've got some news for you, too."

"What news?"

"I'll tell you tomorrow."

"Seven?"

"Right. See you then. Bye."

"Bye." Casey hung up the phone. "What a day."

That night, Casey lay in his bed staring at the ceiling as he had done every night since he moved to Elm Grove. Up to this point he had been very angry, about the move to Elm Grove, about the death of his friend, Billy Keith, about Billy's brother, Bobby, insisting that he keep quiet about how Billy was killed and about moving away from his good friends. All that happened in Shorewood was four months ago. It seemed like yesterday. He missed his friends. When he left Shorewood, he vowed never to make any friends to take their place. No one understood how he felt about the gang. They were all good friends, the only ones he ever had.

Casey cried, too. He would never let anyone know about that. Sometimes he just felt sorry for himself and other times it was the overwhelming grief he felt about Billy's death. There were times when he would stare out his bedroom window and watch as a full moon rose in the eastern sky, fairly hypnotized by its reflection on the glassy surface of the ocean. He shut the world out. Only the gentle whisper of the ocean lapping on the shore entered his consciousness and when the moon disappeared above his house he would fall asleep totally exhausted. There were times, too, when he would awaken at sunrise to gaze at the ball of fire rising out of the ocean, listen to the soft whisper of a gentle surf and the mournful cries of seagulls as they searched the barren beach for morsels of food. He never wanted to leave this cocoon he created for himself. His room was the only place he could trust his feelings without fear of someone probing or watching.

Somehow, Lexie was different from everyone else, not because she was a Black girl. She didn't dress like all the girls and she didn't giggle like them, either. He knew that, like in Shorewood, there were many cliques in Elm Grove and as far as he knew, they either rejected Black students outright or avoided them in subtle ways. Lexie seemed older and quite immune to what the other students thought about her. Thinking of Lexie, he went to sleep with a smile on his face, his first smile since Billy Keith's death.

3

Lexie Gets Involved

*D*espite Casey's moodiness, Lexie was impressed. As she rode beside Casey on the way home from the library, she glanced over at him. *He seems like a really nice guy, but I wonder why he gets so moody. I hope I didn't do anything to make him mad at me. I had to open my big mouth and make that lousy comment about him looking like Jonathan. What's wrong with me? I haven't met anyone quite like him before. He was really talkative the first time we walked home, but he avoids talking every time I bring up Anne Robertson. Why did he pick me to talk to? Why is he so curious about her?*

As Lexie walked her bicycle up Sandy Point Road, she could smell smoke coming from the chimney of her house. This was one of the things she liked about living here, so different from San Francisco. They had a fireplace there, but it was fed with gas and rarely used. Here, piles of wood in the yards and smoke rising from the chimneys were a common sight. The crisp, cold air and the smell of smoke were delightful. When she arrived at home, she was still thinking about the day at school, about Casey and Anne Robertson. At least it had been more interesting than other days in Elm Grove.

Lexie's usual pattern, since moving to Elm Grove, was to go home right after school, study, listen to tapes or read. In addition to her school books, she enjoyed fashion and art magazines and books about solving personal problems. She liked just hanging out by herself in her bedroom or taking an occasional walk up to Sandy Point where she enjoyed the views and the fresh air, but there was something missing. She was lonely.

San Francisco's population was far more diverse, generally more tolerant of the wide variety of racial and ethnic backgrounds. It did not take much time for her to realize that Elm Grove was predominantly Caucasian and that Black students were not exactly welcomed with open arms. At the same time, she knew that it took strangers of any persuasion a long time to make friends in New England.

Lexie never heard her parents discuss anything about their racial differences, nor about problems they might have had in their marriage. Interracial marriages were more common on the West Coast, so it never became an issue. In Elm Grove, Lexie wasn't sure if it was an issue or not. Her interaction with Elm Grove residents was too limited to tell. All she was sure of was that both of her parents worked hard and rarely went out to parties or social events. The only barometer Lexie had to go on was the way they acted at home. They were, in fact, quite peaceful and relaxed, never argued or brought up anything unusual about their relationships with themselves or other people. Her mother was insulated from the outside world as she worked at home. She conducted all her business by phone, fax or e-mail. Her father traveled a great deal. Neither of them, for as long as Lexie could remember, ever cultivated any lasting friendships with neighbors. As for other family members, her grandparents on both sides, died several years ago. There were no connections with any other relatives.

For the most part, over the years, Lexie learned to be content with living one day at a time, not create any waves or reach out to too many people, but at times this became quite confusing. Choosing friends with similar interests was very difficult for her in the city. She was torn between wanting close friends and keeping to herself. She did not want to take on what she felt was excess baggage or being committed to any one person or group. The excess baggage was having to listen to other people's troubles when she had no handle on her own, or openly sharing her troubles with another person or group. It was a matter of trust, which she did not dispense freely. Lexie was a private person, but that was a part of her she was ambivalent about.

Lexie longed for a companion, someone her own age, boy or girl, but could not imagine getting serious enough to go steady and all that entailed. The whole idea of falling in love was too mysterious for her to comprehend. As far as groups were concerned, she did not want to be identified with a particular group. She wanted to keep the freedom to move from one group to another without problems.

There was very little to hold Lexie in San Francisco and scant prospects for her to establish new friendships in Elm Grove, but, despite that, Lexie had looked forward to moving. She was convinced that a new place would be better. Any place would be better than what she had experienced so far, but much to her chagrin, she was the same bland person she always was, or at least that was her opinion of herself. She took some comfort and pride in the fact that her mother was a successful Black woman, the first Black woman to receive an award for outstanding art work in a textbook series. Her mother knew how to become successful from her own home without having to relate to too many people and that is what Lexie was after.

Lexie's relationship with Casey, at least at the outset, was very satisfying and she was anxious to see how long it would last. Her main concern now was how to keep things going with him and how to react to him. She liked him very much and she was afraid she might drive him away. Should she be direct and open with him or shy and retiring? His moods kept her off balance, but she liked the way he treated her, more honest than any other person she knew. The Ann Robertson thing was a way to keep in touch, a vehicle through which she could maintain some semblance of companionship without the excess baggage.

Lexie tossed her book bag on the floor by the front door.

"That you, Lexie?" It was her mother in the living room watching television with her father. As usual, they were watching the six o'clock news broadcast with a roaring fire in the fireplace.

How different it was here. Her father inherited a house full of antiques from his parents which furnished their condominium in San Francisco, but there they seemed out of place. Lexie never paid much attention to the fact that many of the items around the house were used in the latter part of the eighteenth century. Here, the antiques fit better, in the house and in the town. Through them, Lexie felt more connected to the historical aspects of Elm Grove. She felt good about that. Anne Robertson helped, too. She saw the smiling face of a young girl who lived a hundred years ago and she felt drawn to her, wondering about Anne's relationship with Jonathan and how Jonathan must have felt when the love of his life disappeared without a trace.

"Hi, Mom. Hi, Daddy." Lexie started to go upstairs to her room, but she remembered something. "Daddy, you went to Elm Grove High, right?"

"I graduated from Elm Grove High. Why?"

"Do you remember a plaque at the high school? It was for a girl named Anne Robertson?"

"Sure. But, it was in the old high school building, not this one. How do you know about that?"

"I went up to the high school this afternoon with a new friend I met today. The plaque was there."

"Is she in high school?" asked her mother.

"No, Mom, it's a boy and he's in some of my classes. His name is Casey Miller."

"Miller? I had a classmate in high school named Ed Miller. He married a girl named Julie Amesbury," said her father. "They moved away after graduation, I think to Shorewood up on the North Shore. Never heard about him again."

"Casey moved here from Shorewood a few months ago. Could his mother and father be the ones you know?"

"It's a possibility."

"He lives right around the corner on The Causeway."

"Wouldn't that be strange? I'll have to give them a call. What about Anne Robertson?"

"Casey found an old newspaper clipping about this girl who disappeared, Anne Robertson.

"I remember that. It happened a long time ago."

"It was in 1898. Do you know if they ever found her?"

"If I remember right, they never did find her. The old Robertson house is up the street from here. It's the white house with black trim on the other side of the street."

"What? That was where she lived? I've got to call Casey."

"Ask him if his father remembers Goofy Wentworth."

"Goofy Wentworth. What are you talking about, Bob?" asked Mrs. Wentworth.

"Yeah, Dad, what are you talking about?"

"They used to call me Goofy because of the way I played basketball. Ed Miller will remember. We were both on the varsity. I guess I looked a little crazy out there."

"Dad, I just met Casey today. I'm supposed to tell him my father's name is Goofy? I think I'll wait awhile."

Lexie picked up the phone, then hesitated for a moment. *What am I doing? I shouldn't be calling Casey. He'll think I'm too pushy. No, wait, he's not like that. Or is he? I hate this. OK, I'll do it.*

"Hello, may I speak with Casey, please?" *I sound so formal.*

"Sure, just a minute."

Sounded like a young girl's voice, must have been his sister.

"Hi, Casey. It's me, Lexie."

"Hi, Lexie."

"I was just talking with my parents. My father graduated from Elm Grove High. He says they never found Anne Robertson. And he said that Anne Robertson lived up the street from where I live."

There was a pause in the conversation.

"Hello, are you there?" asked Lexie.

"I'm here."

"Isn't it weird? If it wasn't for Anne Robertson we might not have met, I mean,…Are you mad at me?" Lexie waited for Casey to say something. She couldn't think of anything else to say.

"It has nothing to do with you."

Neither spoke for several seconds.

"Well, I have to go now," said Lexie.

"OK. See you in school. Hey, what about walking to school together?"

"Sure. I'd like that. I'll meet you at the bridge at seven." *Oops, I did it again. Maybe I shouldn't have been so anxious.* Lexie hung up the phone, paused for a moment, then smiled.

"Dad?"

"I'm in here, in the kitchen."

"Do you really think Mr. Miller is the one you know?"

"I don't know for sure, but, it'll be worth a call. You seem interested in Anne Robertson. What's that all about?"

"Not really. Casey just mentioned it." *Maybe it was because it was the first time that anyone, let alone a boy, in Elm Grove took an interest in me.*

"I wouldn't know anything about it," said Mrs. Wentworth. "Your father and I met in California."

"That was a long time ago, too."

"Where did you live, in Elm Grove, I mean, when you were in high school?"

"I lived up in the center, behind the Central School. The only reason I remember Anne Robertson was that my father was a lawyer. He helped a Pritchard family settle an estate problem involving the Robertson house. He said the house had a strange history. The Robertson family moved away after Anne disappeared. The house was abandoned for about five years. It was in bad shape. I think a family named Samuelson bought it and restored it. That case was over twenty years ago. I don't know who owns the place now. Here's the phone directory. There's a listing by streets."

Lexie thumbed through the directory and found Salt Point Road. There were six houses listed. At number sixteen, Lexie's house, the name Pritchard appeared. At number 19, directly across the street, the name Moorehead, D. was listed, followed by the names Mason, Harbaugh, Swenson, and O'Shea at numbers 27, 24, 32 and 36 respectively.

"There's a Pritchard family listed for our house," said Lexie.

"Right. We bought the house from the Pritchard estate. We have a plaque on our front porch. It's an historic building."

"I thought you said the Pritchards bought the Robertson house," said Lexie's mother.

"They did and they lived in it for a while, until they built this house," said Mr. Wentworth. "That was a long time ago. According to my father, the house we're in now was built by Jason Pritchard back in the late 1800's. Wait a minute. We have a book that has the history of these houses. As a matter of fact, Anne's father, Clive Robertson, was the first editor of the book. He was the head of the Historical Society and this book has been published every three years since he started it." Lexie's father went to a bookshelf. He selected a thick paperback book entitled, "Historical Homes of Elm Grove" prepared by the Elm Grove Historical Society. He opened the book and looked in the Table of Contents for the Pritchard House. Each chapter explained the origins of a house followed by a time sequence arranged like a family tree showing the changes in ownership and any important events that were associated with the house.

"Here it is. It lists the oldest houses in Elm Grove from the early 1700's to 1995."

"Number 19 must be Dorothy Moorehead's house. She's the librarian," said Lexie.

"What's so strange about that?" asked Mr. Wentworth.

"Nothing, I guess. It just seems weird that we were in the library today and her name turns up. Is there anything about our house?"

"The book says our house was built by Jason Pritchard in 1893, sold to a Hoover family in 1920, then bought by an Allen Pritchard in 1959. There are no other owners listed. As I said, we bought it from the Allen Pritchard estate."

"We found out today that Jonathan Pritchard must have been Anne's boyfriend. It was in the old yearbook. Jonathan must have lived in our house?"

"Looks like it. I remember something my father talked about. I think the Robertson family accused somebody in the Pritchard family of being responsible for Anne's disappearance, something about Jonathan being a close friend. The two families had quite a feud for a while."

"Anything else?" asked Lexie.

"That's all I remember."

Lexie turned a page and found the history of the Robertson house. Less than a year after Anne's disappearance her house was sold to a man named James Samuelson. For a few generations, the house remained in the Samuelson family, but, after World War II, it changed hands several times. The current listing, at number 27, was in the name of the estate of Emily and John Mason.

"What does the estate of Emily and John Mason mean, Daddy?"

"The owners of the house died. It takes a while to settle an estate with property like that. The heirs may be listing it to be sold or they may be keeping it for rental. There can be complications if there was no will."

"You said we bought our house from an estate."

"Right, the Allen Pritchard estate. We looked into buying the Mason's house, but it wasn't for sale. It was still tied up in probate."

"That's enough for one day," said Lexie. "I can't take any more of this."

"Supper will be ready in about fifteen minutes," said Lexie's mother.

"OK, Mom. Gee, tonight I get to eat with Goofy."

Lexie's father smiled. "I guess I'll never live that down."

"We're going out to pick out our Christmas tree tomorrow night. Want to come?" asked Mrs. Wentworth.

"No, Mom, Casey asked me out."

Lexie wasn't sure if Casey would ask her out, but she blurted out her answer as if it was inevitable. It wouldn't hurt to keep her schedule open. She retrieved her book bag and went upstairs to freshen up for dinner. Her bedroom was in the front corner of the house. After washing up she looked out her bedroom window and stared in the direction of the house that Anne Robertson had lived in. It was too dark to see it. There were only six houses on Sandy Point Road and only Lexie's and Dorothy Moorehead's were occupied during the winter. The old Samuelson house and three other houses on the street were boarded up for the Winter. Lexie noticed that the porch lights were on at Dorothy Moorehead's house. Lexie had not paid any attention to the Samuelson house, but, now, it took on an air of mystery. Anne Robertson once lived there.

"Jonathan may have looked out this very window," Lexie muttered to herself. "Casey is going to love this."

It was not only the excitement of finding out something new, it gave Lexie an excuse to call Casey.

"Supper's ready!" Her mother's voice startled her. She fairly flew down the stairs to supper. Her interest in Casey's mystery girl was more than she had thought possible.

"What is your friend like?" asked Lexie's father.

"I don't know him very well, yet. He's nice."

"I remember his father very well. Ed Miller was a quiet sort. He played in three sports, but always found time to go fishing. The few times I went out with him convinced me that I wasn't cut out to be a fisherman, but Ed definitely was. He loved the ocean. We sat for hours out there and he hardly said a word, accept to tell me what to do."

"Casey's a little like that, I guess. He seems to have a lot on his mind. The kids at school think he's a real grouch."

"Why is that?" asked her mother.

"He looks mad all the time, never talks with anyone. I think I was the first one he's talked to at school."

"Why did he pick you out?" asked her father.

"We both got assigned these old closets for us to use as a locker. He looked sad at first. After he found the article, he just wanted to show it to me. He's really not like the kids think he is. He's nice."

"You never know about people," said Mr. Wentworth. "No one's been able to solve the Anne Robertson thing for almost one hundred years. Why so much interest in that?"

"I don't know," said Lexie.

Lexie started to go upstairs to her room, but she paused for a moment. She turned the light on the front porch and stepped outside. There it was, a bronze plaque inscribed with "Pritchard House, 1893." She reached out and touched it. A stiff, cold breeze blew across the porch sending shivers through her. Quickly, she went back into the house and up to her room. It was quite a day.

4

A Close Call

---

*C*asey got to the bridge first. He looked at his watch. It was six fifty-five. He saw Lexie coming down the hill from Sandy Point. Both were bundled up in their winter jackets and, as they fell into line with each other, a blast of cold air caught them unexpectedly. Without thinking, Casey put his arm around Lexie and pulled her close to help shield her from the cold blast of air. Lexie made no motion to stop him. They walked that way along the stretch of road from the bridge to Pritchard's Corner. That stretch was always windy and cold at that time of year, but today it seemed much colder. There were no trees to interrupt the constant icy breeze that blew across the salt marsh.

"Isn't it weird about the ring my mother bought?" asked Casey.

"That is weird. It's weird that it turned up on the same day you found the other one."

"What's your big news?"

"I thought you'd never ask. I found out last night that I live in Jonathan Pritchard's house, in fact, there's a plaque on our front porch that says it was built in 1893. My room may be the one Jonathan had. The house that Anne Robertson lived in is up the street. I can see it from my bedroom window and you'll never guess who lives across from me."

"I give up."

"Dorothy Moorehead."

"What about Anne's house?"

"A family named Samuelson bought it from the Robertsons a long time ago. Some estate owns it now."

"How did you find all this out?"

"We have a phone book with all the latest listings by street. My father showed me another book. The historical society has a list of all the old houses in Elm Grove."

"Did you see my house? We've got a brass plate on our front door that says Colby House."

"I didn't think to look."

They walked on in silence, not really knowing what they had put together. When they reached the intersection at the beginning of The Causeway they stopped and looked at the statue of Jason Pritchard and Casey let go of Lexie.

"I never paid attention to this statue, until now," said Lexie. She was a little disappointed that Casey had backed away from her.

"I didn't either. Look at the dates. He was born in 1843 and died in 1901. He was only fifty-eight years old when he died and it was only three years after Anne's disappearance."

"Are you thinking there's a connection?" There was a distinct tone of sarcasm in her voice which surprised Casey.

"No connection. Don't get upset. I just had a thought, that's all."

"You and your thoughts. You're going to drive me crazy. You keep bringing up things and then you leave me hanging. Wait, I'm sorry. I didn't mean to snap."

"I'm going back to the library tonight. Want to go?" asked Casey.

"There you go again. I can guess what for," said Lexie. "What makes you think you can find answers that nobody else could? Do you think you'll find out what happened to her?"

"No, I'm not that smart. I just have a feeling, that's all. I thought it might be something to do."

"Sorry. I didn't mean to snap at you again. Actually, I like this kind of stuff, too. If we don't find anything more, what will you do?"

"Stay in bed for a week, I guess. Probably suck my thumb, too."

"Yeah, right. I have an errand to run for my mother after school, but if it's OK with you I'll meet you at the bridge at seven tonight."

"I was thinking that myself. We don't have any classes together today, so I'll see you at the bridge at seven."

"Right." *That takes care of my library date. I won't be picking out a Christmas tree.*

Casey's and Lexie's curiosity was increasing, especially since they now had two rings to think about, the plaque at the high school, the news item and, although not so strange, the coincidence of Dorothy Moorehead living across the street from Lexie. It was amazing how pieces of a puzzle were turning up, like finding out where Ann Robertson lived and that Jonathan lived in Lexie's house. They were able to find out that Jonathan Pritchard was Anne's boyfriend, but there was no other trail to follow. At least they didn't think so. Maybe there was more. Casey went through his usual routine when he got home. He could hardly wait to meet Lexie again.

*　　　　　*　　　　　*

The church bells in St. Mary's Church tower tolled seven times when Casey arrived at Salt Marsh Bridge. He leaned his bicycle against the bridge wall and, for a few minutes before Lexie rode up, Casey looked out over salt marsh at the harbor lights. Further, up Old Country Lane, the houses were heavily decorated with Christmas lights and lawn displays. The town's Christmas tree across from the statue of Jason Pritchard was lit. All that was missing was the New England snow. He glanced up at the thickening cloud cover. It hadn't snowed the previous nights as he thought it would. A bitter cold, damp breeze briskly blew across the marsh causing Casey to shiver. The crisp afternoon breezes continued at nightfall, so the wind chill factor was even worse when the sun went down.

"Hi, Casey."

"Hi, Lexie."

"You look like you're in outer space."

"I feel like it sometimes."

They rode slowly, side by side. Neither Casey nor Lexie spoke. The street lamps along Old Country Lane burned dimly with an eerie pumpkin-color in stark contrast to the bright red, green, blue and white Christmas lights that people decorated their houses with along the gutters and on bushes and trees.

"This place still gives me the creeps, even with Santa Claus on the door," said Lexie.

Together Casey and Lexie pulled open the heavy oak door, then the inner door and stepped into the large main room. Casey grabbed Lexie's arm and stopped her.

He whispered to Lexie. "Let's ask Ms. Moorehead for information about 1898, but let's not tell her why we want to know, like the last time."

Lexie nodded. "Do you think she knows anything about this?"

"Maybe, but why would she want to know? It's just a gut feeling. Let's just keep it to ourselves for now. Let me do the talking."

As Casey spoke, he turned to walk toward the main checkout counter. At that moment, Jake Colby, the library custodian, came by with his mop. Casey and Jake collided. Briefly, Casey and Jake's eyes met. Casey could not help but notice Jake's grayish brown, thick eyebrows and steely blue eyes that stared menacingly at him. He was partially bald and had a long scar on the right side of his face that ran from a corner of his mouth to his right ear. He was dressed in baggy, wool pants with a faded plaid flannel shirt that looked like it was two sizes too large. His unkempt appearance and the scowl on his face made him more menacing. There was no mistaking a pungent body odor. With nothing more than a low groan, Jake kept going.

"Sorry," Casey said.

Casey looked at Lexie and shrugged his shoulders.

Jake said nothing. He kept walking as if nothing had happened, pushing a long-handled dust mop in front of him. When he got to the checkout counter, he glanced angrily at Dorothy Moorehead and disappeared through the cellar door.

"Grouch," said Lexie under her breath.

"It would help if he took a bath once in a while," whispered Casey.

Casey and Lexie approached Dorothy Moorehead. She was busily checking in books with one hand and wiping her nose with a handkerchief with the other.

"Excuse me," Casey said. "We'd like to look at the yearbooks again." At that moment, Jake came through the cellar door, glowered at Casey and Lexie, and wandered off toward the front of the library.

"Very well, I believe you know the way."

Casey led the way into the cellar with Lexie close behind. At the bottom of the stairs Lexie stepped in front of Casey and moved to the place where the yearbooks were stored.

"It's gone. The old yearbook is gone," said Lexie.

Casey shrugged his shoulders. "That's weird. Why would that yearbook be missing?"

"It could be in the book return."

"It would be back on the shelf by now. Let's just cool it for now."

"Maybe we can find something in the town history," said Lexie.

They returned to the main floor and approached Dorothy Moorehead. Neither Casey nor Lexie asked about the missing yearbook.

This time Lexie spoke. "We need some help. Can you tell us where we might find some information about the town in 1898?"

"Yeah, like deaths and places where people lived?" Casey blurted out.

Lexie rolled her eyes and looked up at the ceiling. She poked Casey in the ribs and whispered, "I thought we weren't going to tell her anything."

They were interrupted by Dorothy Moorehead. "The town newspaper donated an extensive microfiche file recently, but I haven't had time to study exactly what we have. I do know that the file dates from the first newspaper published here, back in 1890. You'll find the files in the History section in the big cabinet. The directions for using the microfiche viewer are on the table, over there."

"What's micro fish?" Casey whispered to Lexie.

"It's like they took pictures of the newspapers. It's microfilm. I saw it once back in California." Casey gave Lexie a blank look, then she said, "Never mind, I'll show you."

"I looked in the book return. It was empty," said Casey.

"I didn't see anything on her desk, either."

A long oak cabinet with several wide drawers stood against the west wall of the library. Each of its drawers had a neat white label on it with a range of years imprinted on each label. Casey pulled out the drawer labeled 1890 - 1900. In the drawer were tabs with years printed on them. Behind each tab was a set of small black, cylindrical canisters each containing a roll of film. The month or range of months was neatly typed on a label affixed to each cover. Behind the tab marked 1898 were several canisters.

"Let's see what one looks like," Casey said.

"There's the machine we need," said Lexie.

Next to the cabinet was a formidable looking machine with a clear vinyl cover over it. Casey uncovered the machine. Lexie turned it on and threaded one of the rolls of film from the cannister marked January/February into place. There on the screen were the actual pages of the old weekly newspaper, The Townsman. By moving the film, Casey and Lexie could scan each page. The first headline reported a severe snowstorm on January 27, 1898.

"We're at the beginning of the year," said Lexie. "This may take some time."

"The yearbook is usually printed close to the end of the school year, isn't it? Try April."

Lexie took the cannister for March/April out of the drawer and threaded the film into the machine.

"That's really smart. I didn't think of that."

She moved the film until they could see the death notices. None made note of Anne's death. After scanning several frames, the feature story about Anne's disappearance came up on the screen. The date was Thursday, April 11, 1898. The headline read "Robertson Girl Missing." Casey read the story aloud, but with a subdued voice.

"Eleanor and Clive Robertson notified the police that their seventeen- year-old daughter, Ann Robertson, is missing. Police Chief Jonas Mackey told The Townsman that Anne had not returned to her home after studying at the Lending Library. Her parents say she left her home on Sandy Point Lane at 7:00 p.m. last night. Anna Bailey, Library Attendant, confirmed that Anne was at the library until closing time and that Hiram Kingsley, the library custodian let her out shortly before 9:00 p.m. No one has reported seeing her since that time."

For the next ten weeks, the paper featured stories about a futile search and many unproductive leads. Before they realized it, they had taken five canisters out of the drawer.

"Look here," said Lexie. "They thought she might have been kid-naped and held for ransom." "Here's one that says they thought she was murdered."

"They questioned that fellow, Hiram Kingsley, for hours. He was probably the last person to see Anne alive."

"Jonathan Pritchard was her boyfriend. There it is, Lexie. They thought he might have killed her."

"And here's an item that says she might have run away from home. I wonder why they would have thought that."

"Look at that headline. It's six months after she disappeared. 'Robertson Girl Presumed Dead.' They didn't find her," said Casey. "There's the article I found in my locker. It's dated October 21, 1898"

There was a list of prominent people there at the memorial service. According to the article, Oliver Colby gave a moving speech praising Anne's virtues. He suggested that they might name the new lending library in her honor, but apparently that had no effect.

"That didn't happen," said Lexie, pointing to the last sentence in the article. "According to this article, the name of this place was the Colby-Pritchard Lending Library."

"He was probably just saying something to make her family feel better."

Casey and Lexie now had reams of information about Anne Robertson, all revealed in various news items dating from April 1898. The last one referring to Anne appeared on November 15, 1898. Anne's father, Clive, owned and operated the only department store in the town. His descendants founded Elm Grove and Clive started the Elm Grove Historical Society.

Anne's boyfriend was Jonathan Morgan Pritchard. Jonathan, according to his mother, was at home on the night Anne disappeared. Jason Pritchard, Jonathan's father, was in the city. Jonathan's father was a wealthy landowner and developer and one of the founders of the Elm Grove Lending Library. He and his partner, Oliver Colby, donated the land and the money to build the library, which was under construction at the time of Anne Robertson's death. There was also a description of Anne's probable route from the library to her home.

"She took the same route that we take to get home from here," whispered Lexie.

"Look at this article," said Casey. He read part of it aloud. "The night Anne disappeared it started to rain heavily at about 8:00 p.m. She probably delayed leaving for home to wait for the rain to stop. It rained all night, so officials believe she had to leave the library at closing time. The route Anne took on was dark and the unpaved road was muddy."

"Jonathan Morgan Pritchard really was Anne's boyfriend," sighed Lexie. "Just think. I live in his house. Maybe I sleep in the same room he did."

"Then he must have used my locker, or closet, or whatever that is."

"And put the news item there. We'll probably never know how the ring got there."

"Here's an article about Anne's father," said Lexie. "It's dated before Ann disappeared."

Lexie read the article out loud.

Robertson Objects to Library Site

Clive Robertson, Chairman of the Elm Grove Historical Society, made his views known last night at the Town Meeting. The Society is objecting to the building of a lending library on the site they say was formerly an Indian burial ground. He requested that the Town issue an order to cease construction until an investigation is made into the historical significance of artifacts found at the site. When asked by Jason Pritchard what evidence there was, Mr. Robertson showed some artifacts which he says are indicative of those found at Indian grave sites. Oliver Colby, Pritchard's business partner, told the Town Meeting that there was no legal way the Town could stop them from building on the site. However, he added that if any artifacts are found during construction, they will be turned over to the Historical Society. The meeting was adjourned after Colby and Pritchard were given approval for the building. After the meeting, Mr. Robertson expressed his profound dismay at the decision and accused Colby and Pritchard of underhanded tactics.

Lexie turned the knob on the machine and advanced the film. She stopped at an article dated March 21, 1898. Casey read this one:

Clive Robertson Resigns

Clive Robertson, Chairman of the Elm Grove Historical Society, resigned yesterday as Chairman and announced that he was officially ending his affiliation with the society. Mr. Robertson stated, "I believe the society has surrendered its independence as an advocate for historical preservation. Members consistently vote to approve the desecration of historical sites in favor of the Colby-Pritchard Construction Company. I have nothing more to say." The members accepted Mr. Robertson's resignation with regret.

"My father said that there was a big thing going on between the Robertsons and Pritchards. Now I know why," said Lexie. "He said he thought the Robertsons accused Jonathan Pritchard of being responsible for Anne's death."

"What about the ring my mother bought?"

Casey felt a little queasy and nervous. His stomach growled and he gripped it trying to make it stop. *Did Jonathan know what happened to Anne, like he knew what happened to Billy? Did he keep quiet, too?*

"Are you OK?" asked Lexie.

Casey felt like the floor disappeared from under him. He felt dizzy. He heard a voice that sounded like someone yelling into a barrel. It was the same feeling he had on the morning he found out about Billy Keith's death. Billy and Bobby lived across the street and when he saw the police cars and ambulance at the Keith's house he went over to see what had happened. Billy's mother had passed out when she got the news and the whole scene in the Keith home had turned into chaos. It seemed to Casey like some kind of weird dream. He would wake up and he would be safe at home. But, this was real and very hard to accept. The move to Elm Grove happened so fast that he did not have a chance to work things out with Bobby and the rest of The Sandbox Gang.

"Casey, snap out of it. You're making me nervous."

"What's the matter?" he asked.

"You looked like you passed out. Are you OK?"

"Sure, I'm OK. I just felt dizzy for a minute." He pulled himself together and put the canisters back in the file.

"Now what," said Lexie.

They sat quietly for a moment. Suddenly, a loud thump broke the silence. It was Jake Colby again, mopping the floor. He hit his mop handle on a leg of the table where Casey and Lexie were looking at the screen. Casey and Lexie were so lost in thought that they failed to hear or see Jake approach. Jake mumbled a few words and continued his way.

"What did he say?" whispered Lexie.

"I don't know, but I don't think it was 'excuse me.'"

"He gives me the creeps, too."

"Are you done here?" asked Casey.

"Not really, but, it's after eight. I should be getting home."

"I have to stop at the Harbor Market. I'll ride with you to the bridge."

At the bridge, Lexie stopped her bike and turned to Casey. "Are you OK? You looked really pale at the library. Is there something I should know about?"

"It's nothing. Don't worry about it."

Casey knew it was not as simple as that. It was four months since Billy died and he wished he could get back to normal. He wasn't sure what normal was anymore.

Lexie continued toward her home. Casey turned back and rode to the market at the Harbor Mall. He bought a gallon of milk. It was a moonless, overcast night. Once Casey turned onto The Causeway and got beyond the lighted Christmas tree, he could barely make out the pavement in front of him.

As Casey approached Salt Marsh Bridge, a car's headlights flashed behind him projecting his own shadow ahead of him, but helping to light his way. Bicycle riders were very common on the beach roads, even at night. Usually, people driving cars were very careful, so it did not occur to Casey that as long as he stayed close to the edge of the road anything would happen. On instinct, he looked behind him and realized that he was in the car's path. He had to act quickly. He could ride as hard as he could to get to the other side of the bridge, but he if he didn't make it he would not be able to maneuver on the narrow bridge. He had nowhere to go except to stay close to the shoulder of the road. As Casey looked back, his front wheel struck soft sand. His bike stopped abruptly and Casey pitched forward into the ice cold, wet and muddy salt marsh. The car missed him by inches. He felt a sharp pain where the handlebars jammed into his ribs. He lay in darkness soaked to the skin and shivering from the cold. His bike was a few feet away with the milk beside it. The car was gone.

Casey rose slowly, thankful he was still alive, but his right side ached where the bicycle handlebars jabbed him. His ski jacket helped absorb part of the blow, but it was painful to breathe. The front wheel of his bicycle was twisted like a pretzel. He paused for a moment in the pitch black darkness, waiting to see if the car was going to return. This road was the only access to the beach. Suddenly, a car's headlights approached from the opposite direction and in seconds the car passed Casey and sped off toward St. Mary's Church at Pritchard's Corner. Whoever it was must have parked somewhere near the church, waiting for Casey to come by. This someone had to know Casey would ride by there at this time.

Casey raised himself, forced himself to stand and made his way back onto the road, dragging his bicycle behind him.

"Brrrr, I'm freezing. I've got to get home."

Painfully, with the milk in his hand, he threw his bicycle over his shoulder and crossed the bridge. He turned and looked toward the church. A car was parked about two hundred yards away under the street lamp at Pritchard's Corner. The engine was running and the headlights were out. Casey could see the exhaust fumes in the light. Casey rushed as fast as he could to get off the road. He stumbled onto the sand in front of the first beach house and fell forward onto his bicycle. The pain in his chest was excruciating. He lay in the darkness and twisted his body so he could look in the direction of the church. He could still see the exhaust from the car rising into the glare of the street lamp. Suddenly, the car's headlights came on and the car drove away, disappearing down Wood Road.

The cold sand and an icy cold breeze numbed Casey's body. He had never been so cold in his life. He got back to the street and trudged homeward, looking behind him frequently to assure himself that he wasn't being followed. Dizzy from the pain in his ribs he took one last look toward Salt Marsh Bridge before he opened the door to the cellar.

Casey turned the light on in the cellar and stowed his bicycle along the cellar wall.

"Look at me. I'm a mess, and look at that wheel," he muttered to himself. "I can't let the family see me like this. They'd have a fit."

Stealthily, he made his way up the stairs to the kitchen and with as little noise as possible, wiped the sand off the milk container and put the milk in the refrigerator. He could hear the television in the living room. Quietly, without announcing himself, he went unnoticed up the stairs. Kathy's door was shut. He could see her light under the door. Carefully, he opened the door to his room, stepped in, and slowly closed it behind him. He took off his dirty clothes and hid them on the floor in his closet. *I'll wash them when I'm alone in the house.* He put on a bathrobe and gathered up what he usually slept in, a Celtics T-shirt and dark blue sweat pants with the letters YALE imprinted down the left leg. No one in the family went to Yale. Casey's sister Kathy got them for his last birthday. She said, "Maybe the Yale will rub off on you."

He quietly strode down the hall to the bathroom. There he took a quick look at the bruise on his ribs and took a hot shower. It took great effort to apply his soap. Every movement produced a pain so sharp that he thought he would pass out.

A short time later, Casey went downstairs and gingerly waved to his parents hoping they would not notice his face as he winced from the pain.

"Hi, Mom. Hi, Pop."

His father lifted his right arm as if it was being pulled by a puppet string. Both of his parents were too engrossed in a television program to notice anything strange going on.

Casey decided to call Lexie from the telephone in the kitchen.

"Lexie! Someone tried to run me over after I left you." Casey whispered into the phone.

"Did you see who it was?" Lexie asked.

"No, it was too dark and it happened too fast. Do you think it has anything to do with the Anne Robertson thing?"

"Maybe it was just someone who didn't see you. Maybe it was a drunk," Lexie replied. "Are you OK? You didn't look too good at the library, now you must be a basket case."

"I've got sore ribs. Whoever it was really meant it. I'm sure he saw me. He waited in front of the church and then drove away when I hid on the beach. If I hadn't looked back and gone into the ditch I would have been killed.

"Did you see what kind of car it was?"

"It looked like a station wagon, but I was too far off the road when I landed and then too far away to make out what kind it was. My bike is a wreck, but it's just the front wheel that's busted. It's a good thing I've got a spare."

"I'll talk to you in the morning on the way to school. See you at seven?"

"OK. See you then."

Casey returned to his room. Ordinarily, he would have raided the refrigerator, but, tonight, his stomach felt queasy from the pain in his ribs. Why would anyone purposely try to run him down? He decided not to say anything to his parents. After inspecting the damage to his ribs, again, and satisfied that it was just a bad bruise, he lay on his bed for an hour re-living the events of the night. Exhausted, he pulled his blankets over his head and drifted off to sleep.

5

A Mysterious Box

"Get up, Casey, it's time for school."

His mother's voice from the kitchen sounded more emphatic than usual. He pulled two layers of thick blankets tightly over his head and rolled over to face his bedroom wall.

"Ow!" he grunted. Half asleep, he had forgotten his bruised ribs.

"I need a little more sleep," Casey mumbled, but then he remembered that he was meeting Lexie at Salt Marsh Bridge.

"Get up, Casey,"

It would have been the same scene repeated since winter began had he not told Lexie he was meeting her. Casey normally would cling desperately to his warm blankets and he would not let his brain offer any help to open his eyelids, but the thought of meeting Lexie gave him the motivation to move. He was far from being bright-eyed and bushy-tailed, but his movements were animated by comparison to his normal routine.

"All right, I'm up."

Casey sat on the edge of his bed, rubbed his eyes and stretched his arms toward the ceiling. A sharp pain in his bruised ribs caused him to jerk his arms down. "Ow. Can't we get some heat up here? I'm freezing."

The only heat for his room was from a single hot air vent connected to the furnace in the cellar, but the vent was rusted shut half way, so he was not getting his share of the heat. As he stumbled toward the bathroom, he heard his mother shout. "Casey Miller, where are you? Your breakfast is ready. I can't wait here all day. I'm going to be late for work."

"OK, I'm up." He stumbled into the bathroom still half asleep.

Every morning, the pleasant smell of freshly toasted bread and rich aromas of hot cocoa and coffee rose from the kitchen below. In Shorewood it was like that, too, when winter came on.

Casey looked in the bathroom mirror. Every sandy blond hair on his head was pointing in a different direction. He squinted at the freckle-faced image that peered back at him, looking for any signs of blemishes. He was grateful that none had appeared. He splashed water on his face then bared his teeth at the mirror, grabbed his toothbrush and squeezed out a dab of toothpaste and began brushing.

"Ouch," he cried aloud.

He lifted his T-shirt on the right side and lightly touched a large purplish-red bruise on his ribs, then stumbled, still half asleep, back to his room where he squeezed into a pair of faded jeans. As he pulled on a sweatshirt, another flash of pain caused him to cry out. Back in the bathroom, he wet his hands and ran his fingers through his hair, careful not to raise his arm too high. He stared straight into his own eyes for a moment and gingerly combed his hair.

With a pair of worn out Nike running shoes and gray sweat socks in his hand, Casey padded his way, barefoot, down the stairs and into the kitchen. He took a deep breath and inhaled the warm air and the smell of the kitchen. His mother had her coat on.

"Your sister left a few minutes ago, your father left two hours ago and I'm leaving now. Did you sleep well last night? You look tired," said his mother. "There's toast and cocoa on the table."

"I'm OK, Mom. Go. I'll be fine." Casey was not going to mention a word about last night. He would wait until his mother left the house before he attempted to put his shoes and socks on. It was going to hurt to do that.

His mother hollered back at him as she went down the front steps. "If you go anywhere after school, remember to leave us a note,"

It really wasn't necessary to say so. Since he moved to Elm Grove, Casey always came directly home from school, mainly because he had no place else to go. He was content to stay by himself. His usual activity after school was a lonely walk on the beach, settling down with a good mystery story or losing himself in his Walkman radio, shutting out the world with his headset. He had no favorite music, just loud. Last summer was different. He was always busy. He spent the end of the summer working as a deck hand with his father. His father got him the job before they moved to Elm Grove. He guessed his father thought it would help him forget what happened to Billy. It helped keep him occupied, but it certainly could not make him forget.

Now that he lived in Elm Grove, Casey had few outlets for his energy and, so, in the last four months, his only exercise consisted of riding his bike or walking to and from school and occasionally running on the beach. He had no friends in Elm Grove, because of his belligerent attitude. He refused to talk to anyone about what he was feeling. His world came unglued with Billy's death. He missed the regular routine of meeting with his friends and horsing around with Billy. He withdrew from his sister, Kathy, too. Now, she was upset with him. Meeting and talking with Lexie was helping to defrost the coldness he felt toward everyone. At the same time, Lexie did not give in to him or press him or feel sorry for him and, for that matter, push him away or avoid him. He had given her plenty of reasons to walk away, yet she was still willing to go along with whatever he threw at her.

The clock over the kitchen sink read six forty-five. Painfully, he pulled on his socks. He swallowed the last of the toast and cocoa, while shoving his feet into his well-worn shoes. It hurt even to lift his foot to a chair and bend to tie the laces. He poked his arms into his nylon jacket, grabbed a foil-wrapped sandwich and plodded off to meet Lexie. at Salt Marsh Bridge.

A few minutes earlier the sun had broken through dark clouds on the horizon casting brilliant colors in the sky to the East. Above him the sky was completely overcast with a gray coating of moist, threatening clouds. It was another damp, cold, but windless December day.

A lone figure was standing on the bridge, bundled up with a hood and a scarf, so he couldn't see a face.

"Lexie?" Casey yelled. She waved her arm. It was too cold to talk. She fell into line beside Casey.

After several minutes, Casey said, "You haven't asked me about last night."

"Sorry, I'm too cold to talk. Anyway, are you sure it wasn't an accident, or something? You're making me nervous, again," Lexie said.

"I thought about it a lot last night and I'm pretty sure it was on purpose. Do you think it might have something to do with Anne Robertson?'

"I don't know," said Lexie.

They walked on in silence.

"Isn't it weird about the yearbook disappearing, right after we looked at it?" asked Casey a few moments later.

Lexie mumbled a reply. They continued on in silence.

"Jake Colby acted strange, too. Did you see the look he gave Dorothy Moorehead?"

"I saw the look he gave us," said Lexie.

When they arrived at school, Casey held the door open for Lexie and both welcomed the warmth of the hallway. They stowed their belongings in their closets and went their separate ways to their first class. They met later in their English class. Lexie sat in front and to the right of Casey. He spent the whole class time staring at her. He had a lot on his mind. He was desperately trying to forget his friends in Shorewood, especially Billy Keith. The pain in his ribs nagged at him making it difficult to find a comfortable sitting position in desk chair.. No matter how he tried he could not let go of the Anne Robertson thing and he wondered if he hadn't gone too far in getting Lexie involved. Maybe he should stop this now. If someone really tried to run him over, Lexie was in danger, too. Beyond that, was Lexie becoming his friend? Should he keep seeing her? Would she go away, too, like Billy did?

At the end of the day, Casey met Lexie at their closets.

"TGIF, right?" asked Lexie.

"That's for sure."

"What are you doing this weekend?"

"Nothing much. My parents will be away tomorrow at a wedding up in Shorewood and Kathy is going skating. Do you want to see my bike?," Casey asked. Casey held his breath. *What am I doing? She's going to think I'm crazy."*

"Sure, I'll be over around eleven," Lexie replied

"Mind if I walk home with you?"

Lexie smiled. "You didn't have to ask."

Neither spoke until they said goodbye at Salt Marsh Bridge.

*   *   *

For nearly two centuries the land on which Casey's house was built was called Moss Island by early settlers who made their living gathering Irish moss, which was and still is used in food products. In 1893, Oliver Colby and his partner Jason Pritchard bought the island in a suspicious deal involving the state legislature. The legislature used an obscure homestead law to overturn the decision of the town fathers who opposed the purchase. Oliver and Jason, proceeded to ban the Irish mossers which deprived them of the means of making a living that their ancestors had used since they arrived in Elmwood many years before. Oliver and Jason divided ownership of the island between them. After that, again over the objections of the townspeople, Oliver sold back a portion of the land he owned called Admiral's Point, short for Admiral Hiram Billingsley Point, named for an Elm Grove citizen who served in the initial years of the U.S. Navy. He sold it to the federal government which subsequently built the Coast Guard Station. Oliver argued that the sale would provide the area with official Coast Guard oversight and save thousands of lives, but from that point on, the Colby-Pritchard partnership was looked upon as nothing short of traitorous. To make matters worse, improvements to The Causeway were made at the expense of the federal government. One year later, Oliver built his house and changed the name of his section of the island, Colby Shore, but the town never adopted that name. A short time later, Oliver built three additional houses which were sold to members of the state legislature.

The southern section of the island was called Sandy Point where Jason Pritchard built his house, the one purchased by Lexie's parents. Apparently, he did not share the huge profits personally generated by Oliver. In the year 1900, the partnership was dissolved following a legal battle that lasted four years. One year after that Jason died.

Saturdays in December were lonely times on the beach. Sometimes a few bicyclists would go by, but snow and icy winds would soon put a stop to that. Across the street from Casey's house, a few people braved the cold weather to work on their boats in the boatyard. From the kitchen in Casey's house he could hear the familiar sound of pounding hammers and whirring sanders. Surely, this would be the last weekend for boat repairs. Boats of all shapes and sizes stood in dry-dock in wooden racks. It would be several months before their masters put them back in the water.

At ten-thirty on Saturday morning, after his family left, Casey walked to the five-foot sea wall behind his house. Army engineers built the wall to protect the beach houses from the surge of the ocean. He propped his elbows on the top of the wall. With his chin in his hands, he stared at the vast ocean and observed that it was low tide. He took deep breaths of the salty ocean air, again being careful not to stretch his ribs too far. He smelled the pungent, distinctive odor of seaweed.

The highest point on Moss Island was Admiral's Point. about fifty feet above the ocean. At its foot, boulders as large as Sherman tanks deflected the heavy blasts of surf and protected that point of land from erosion. From Casey's position at the sea wall, to his left, he had an unobstructed view of the huge waves which broke against the base of Admiral's Point.

"Hmmm, I love low tide. Sure beats breathing school air all day."

Casey's thoughts drifted back to the months before he moved to Elm Grove. Last Spring, three months before Billy Keith's death, things changed drastically for The Sandbox Gang. The gang members stole some tomatoes from a garden adjoining the playground. All of them lied to the police when asked the names of the ones who were there, but eventually all had to pay a share for the tomatoes. Because of that incident the police became more vigilant and The Sandbox Gang was forced to keep a low profile. In April, two of the members, twin brothers, Tony and Angie Juliani set fire to the Prospect Hill camp ground. That was determined accidental and there were no repercussions from that, but on a fateful night in mid May, Tony and Angie broke into the Ellis School. They broke a small cellar window, squeezed through and dropped about six feet to the cellar floor. They dowsed a barrel full of papers with lighter fluid and set fire to it. When they tried to get out, they found that the window was too high for them to reach. So, they ran upstairs. They didn't know that they had set off a silent burglar alarm. In the meantime, the heat from the fire set off the fire alarm. By the time they reached the street, fire engines, ambulances and police cruisers were only minutes from the school. A police cruiser just happened to be patrolling close by and so Tony and Angie were caught running up the street.

Two days later, three police cars, with lights flashing, drove across the Ellis Playground and pulled up to The Sandbox . Except for Tony and Angie, the gang was there. No one moved. The biggest policeman Casey had ever seen got out of the lead car. He was "Gooseneck". It was a nickname given to him many years ago mostly because he had a long, muscular neck. After questioning everyone, the gang members were ordered into the police cars. Casey went alone with Gooseneck. He sat in the back and felt the powerful surge of the police car's engine as it propelled the car across the playground, onto the street and up Casey's street to his house. Casey would never forget the fear he felt, not knowing what to expect when he faced his parents, but it was the sound and feeling of the powerful cruiser that impressed him most. Gooseneck stopped the car in front of his house. He got out and opened the door for Casey.

"Get out," he said. "Come with me."

Casey never knew what the impact his being brought home by Gooseneck would be on his family. He and his father were close, even though his father didn't have too much time to spend with him.

"I need to talk to you alone," said Gooseneck to his father.

"Go upstairs, Casey," said his father.

Casey went upstairs and listened as hard as he could to hear what Gooseneck and his father were saying, but he could only hear mumbling from the living room. After about ten minutes, Gooseneck left. Casey's father came up the stairs.

In a few short words, his father said, "No more Sandbox. Do you understand?"

Casey didn't go back to The Sandbox and what transpired a short time later put an end to The Sandbox Gang forever. He remembered the date and time very well. At 1:00 a.m. on Thursday, August 18 he was awakened by the slamming of a car door. Colored lights danced on the ceiling of his bedroom. From his upstairs window he saw a police car, lights flashing, parked across the street in front of Billy Keith's house. One policeman stood by the car while the other, whom he recognized as

Gooseneck by his size, rang the doorbell at the Keith's house. The porch light came on. Gooseneck went in. Casey was riveted to his window. After only a few minutes, Gooseneck came out and Mr. and Mrs. Keith followed. They got into the police car and Casey watched the flashing lights of the cruiser until it turned left at the end of the block and disappeared around the corner. Casey was so tired he went to sleep as soon as his head hit his pillow.

Casey was awakened by bright sunlight streaming through his bedroom. He looked out the window, again. Cars were parked everywhere up and down the street and more were arriving. Quickly, Casey got dressed and ran across the street. The Keith's front door was open, so he walked in along with other people. Casey was familiar with the house. He had been there many times over the years. He pushed his way through a crowd of people looking for Billy or Bobby or anyone he knew. He found Bobby alone sitting at a picnic table in his back yard, his face shielded by his arms. His body trembled from his sobbing. He looked up at Casey. His eyes were red and his face was wet from his tears. His bright red hair was matted and his clothes disheveled.

"He's dead. Billy's dead."

The news hit Casey like a slap in the face.

"What happened?"

"Rosie killed him at the Barker Lumber."

Casey was stunned. Bobby got up and dragged him by the arm to a remote corner of the back yard.

"Billy, Rosie, Donny and me, we climbed the fence. We were running across the roof, you know, the long one by the fence. Anyway, Billy slipped and fell. We heard him crying. I thought he said, "Run." Donny and I got scared. I figured Billy could take care of himself. We ran and left him there, but Rosie went back. Somebody heard us and called the police. We got away, but they found Billy. They say he bled to death from a blow to the head. They think he was murdered. Rosie must have tried to shut him up."

"Rosie wouldn't do anything like that," said Casey.

Bobby could barely speak. "I didn't think so either, but the police think Billy was murdered. You can't tell anyone I told you this. They'll come and arrest me. They'll think I killed him. What can I do?"

"Where is Rosie? Is he here?"

"I don't know where he is."

"What about Donny?"

"I don't know where he is either. Why did Rosie do it?" Bobby sobbed out loud and looked up at Casey through bloodshot eyes.

Casey felt like someone had punched him in the face. Bobby and Donny had left Billy to die and Rosie was suspected of murdering him. After all the time they spent together in The Sandbox Gang, how could Rosie, Donny and Bobby let that happen?

Casey tried to comfort him. "You don't know that and you couldn't have known what happened to Billy. It's not your fault."

But, Bobby was inconsolable. "He'd still be alive. You've got to help me. I lied to the police when they asked me if I was there. Promise me you won't tell. It would kill my mother. Since my father died, I've been giving her a lot of grief. I've been in too much trouble already."

To this day, Casey could not explain why, but he said, "Don't worry, Bobby. I won't tell anyone. I promise." Bobby and he returned to the house, but Casey did not stay. He went back to his room, curled up on his bed and cried.

A few days later, Casey attended Billy's funeral. He was in shock. He had known Billy since he was four years old. Three weeks after the funeral, Casey and his family moved to Elm Grove. He didn't speak to Bobby or any of his friends again. The police were investigating, but they had no leads. Everyone in Casey's family was stunned by Billy's death, too, but they were careful not to bring up the subject. Casey could not understand why.

What could Casey do? His only answer was not to trust anyone, keep to himself and nobody would ask any questions or get him in trouble.

The icy cold spray from the crashing waves licked at Casey's face and brought him back to reality. The weather was crisp and cold. A brisk breeze disturbed the ocean's surface. Whitecaps appeared and disappeared like lights flickering on an off in the morning sunlight. The surf was up and the tide was moving in. Casey loved the ocean. He could not imagine living away from it.

"It's really beautiful out here, isn't it?" It was Lexie. She had seen him from the street and approached alongside the house. "We didn't have anything like this in California. You were really in outer space again. Want to talk about it?"

Casey took a moment to compose himself. In those times when he dredged up the whole event, Casey a heavy sadness would come over him leaving him on the verge of tears. How could he keep his promise to Bobby and keep his sanity, too? His best friend's brother left Billy to die, to bleed to death and Rosie may have killed him.

"I said, do you want to talk about it?"

"I was just thinking about my friends back in Shorewood."

"I didn't have many friends in San Francisco, so I don't spend too much time thinking about where I used to live."

"I was a member of a gang. I thought up the name, The Sandbox Gang, just as a joke."

"And you were a drug dealer, right?"

"No, it wasn't anything like that. None of the kids was bad, but there was plenty of trouble. We first met at a place called Ellis Playground in a summer day camp when we were three or four years old. There was this sandbox in one corner of the playground. After the camp closed we met there almost every day. We'd just hang out, tell jokes, and make fun of the younger kids who came down to the playground. Compared to the other gangs around, we were cream-puffs."

"So, you never got into trouble?"

"We all did, a little bit, but it got worse as we got older. All of us came from poor families. There was Tony and Angie Juliani, twin brothers who liked to set fires. They set Prospect Hill Camp Ground on fire and fire engines from five cities had to come and put it out. It was an accident, but nobody believed them. All they did was start a small campfire and it got out of hand. The problem was the campground was closed. They weren't supposed to be there. But, they set fire to a school, too."

"You weren't with them?"

"No, I never went anywhere with them outside The Sandbox. They just got some strange ideas. We never knew what they were going to do. There was Rosario "Rosie" Germano, too. He was fifteen. He had to stay back one year in school. He swore a lot and was always picking fights with people who made fun of his dirty clothes. He lived on Exchange Street. It was a poor neighborhood where a lot of tough older gang members used to hang out mostly to buy and sell drugs. We all knew that Rosie came all the way up to The Sandbox to get away from that drug crowd. There was Donny Nabors, a real great friend. He lived on Exchange Street, too. His family was the only black family in the neighborhood. He was fourteen. He was the quiet one of the group. Randy Morton at age 14 was a better all-round athlete than most of the people at the high school. He could run fast, and play baseball like someone much older. I could never find out why he refused to try out for any of the junior high school teams.

"I knew someone like that in San Francisco. Everyone talked about him, but he never showed up on any teams."

"There were three girls, too; Martha Williams, came from a large family. She had four brothers and four sisters. Becky Shaw was known mostly for the odd clothes she wore, because she always got the hand-me-downs from three older sisters. Lilly Nabors was Donny's sister, a year younger than Donny. She was really shy with anyone outside The Sandbox Gang, but with the gang she always had a joke to tell. All of the girls were fourteen years of age when I left. All of them lived within walking distance of the Ellis Playground."

"What was Billy like?"

"He was my best friend. He was the best boxer. He had the fastest hands and feet I've ever seen. The only problem was no one was brave enough to fight him, so he teased and picked fights with his younger brother, Bobby. Billy was a year older and a lot bigger than the rest of us. Bobby was fourteen, much smaller than Billy so he was no match. Despite the fights, the two brothers were very close. If Billy was alive he'd be sixteen this month."

"You mean Billy died?"

"I didn't mean to talk so much. It must be the salt air. C'mon, I'll show you my bike. It's in the cellar."

"How did Billy die?"

Casey kept walking in silence toward the cellar door. Lexie stood still for a moment watching Casey.

"Are you coming?" asked Casey.

"I guess you're not going to tell me about Billy Keith."

Casey disappeared into the cellar. Lexie followed. By now she was familiar with Casey's moodiness, so she decided to back away and not press for an answer.

"This is a great house," said Lexie. "Look at those walls, all fieldstone. It would take a whopper of a storm to hurt this house."

"It's been standing here for a hundred years. They must have done something right," said Casey. "Are you going to be an architect, or something?"

"Maybe. Look at your bike. You were lucky you didn't get killed. What did your parents say?"

"I haven't told them anything."

"Why not?"

"I just don't want them getting worried. First thing you know I'd be up at South Shore Hospital."

"I know. My parents are like that. What are you going to do now?"

"Fix my bike, I guess."

Casey's spare wheel hung from a nail driven into one the large timbers that held the house up. Lexie reached up and took it down.

"What are you going to do with this?" Lexie said, pointing to an old outboard motor.

"My father's going to fix it for me so I can use it this summer to go fishing or just cruising."

While Casey worked on his bicycle, Lexie's curiosity got the better of her. She moved about the cellar, looked under the canvases and marveled at all the fishing gear. When her curiosity was almost satisfied she noticed a field stone that looked like it was loose. She poked at it and the stone crashed to the floor near Casey's feet.

"We'd better get out of here. You might wreck the whole house."

Casey picked up the stone and tried to put it back. When he raised his arms, he felt a sudden flash of pain.

"Ow," he cried.

"You're hurt," said Lexie.

"It's my ribs."

"Let me do that." Lexie took the stone and tried to feed it back into the hole. As she did, large chips of patching cement fell away widening the hole to about six inches square.

"Stand on this," said Casey. He pulled a large paint can to the wall.

Lexie put the stone down, stood on the paint can and began brushing the loose cement from the hole.

"There's something in there," Lexie said.

"Take my flashlight," said Casey. "I'm having a problem lifting my arms."

Lexie pointed the light into the hole, reached in and pulled out a metal box covered with a white crust.

"It looks important. Do you think we ought to open it?" asked Casey.

"Are you kidding? Do you think I can wait to see what's inside?"

"Hand me that hammer and screwdriver. If I get into trouble, I'll tell them you made me do it."

"They won't believe you, anyway. So, open it."

6

A Revelation and a Break-In

*C*asey chipped away at the white crust. With a few taps with a hammer and a twist of a screwdriver the box popped open. He pulled out a yellowish envelope folded in half and sealed with a circle of wax. Imbedded in the wax seal was the initial C. Casey cut around the wax with a sharp fishing knife and handed Lexie the envelope.

"You read it," said Casey.

Lexie carefully removed a letter from the envelope written in a very fancy long hand in a well-preserved bold black ink.

> Be it known to all those present that I, Oliver L. Colby, being of sound mind, do now confess to a grievous crime. I make this confession willfully under no duress.

> On the night of April 10, 1898, it being a Thursday, one Jason Pritchard, my partner in business, knocked on my door. He was in a frightful state of mind and appearance. He reported to me that, in the blinding rainstorm in progress, moments earlier, his horse killed Anne

Robertson, daughter of Clive and Beatrice Robertson of
this town.

Casey and Lexie stared at each other in disbelief. Lexie continued
reading:

Mr. Pritchard, according to his report, failed to see Miss
Robertson at the intersection of Wood Road and The
Causeway. Mr. Pritchard's horse struck Miss Robertson.
According to Mr. Pritchard, Miss Robertson died by the
roadside of wounds to her head.

On discovering that Miss Robertson had expired, Mr.
Pritchard had a fit of panic. In a moment of desperation,
fearful of the dire consequences of the event on our social
standing and our business partnership, he placed Miss
Robertson's body in his carriage and forthwith transported her to my door. He came to me for advice. I, equally
fearful of the consequences and weak of character, helped
devise a plan to hide Miss Robertson's body so she would
not be found and the incident would not be reported.

On that fateful night, the two of us, in the stormy night,
drove Miss Robertson's body to our lending library now
under construction and buried her there.

Casey and Lexie looked at each other, again. They were speechless. There was more:

> Mr. Pritchard and I took a solemn oath of secrecy, never to reveal this dastardly deed, but, after careful reflection, I fear the worst. We could be ruined if the truth of the matter were revealed. Therefore, in preparation for that event, I have set aside five hundred gold coins for my heirs who have been waiting anxiously for my death to inherit my fortune. Since I have apportioned my estate in a separate will, I have devised a separate plan for the coins. Whichever heir is able to solve the code which follows will find the location of the coins and be entitled to ownership.

21-12-1-13-19—14-15-19-5

> I write this so that the true story of my involvement will be recorded. Should Jason Pritchard, or his successors, reveal the secret, then I have provided my own account.

> I pray that I will receive forgiveness in heaven for my weakness of character.

> Signed, this Twelfth day of April in the year of our blessed Lord, 1898.

> Oliver L. Colby.

Casey and Lexie had unwittingly stumbled on the evidence revealing the reason for the disappearance of Anne Robertson. Anne's death had been covered up by two of the town's most influential men. Even though Anne died almost one hundred years ago, it hit Casey hard. No one had found out about the real circumstances behind Billy Keith's death, either. He was stretching it, but in his mental condition the connection was easy to make. He realized that helping Bobby was part of a cover up, too. Jason Pritchard and Oliver Colby had their reasons, quite different from Bobby's, but the result, Casey felt, was the same. Like Oliver Colby, Casey became a willing partner in Bobby's cover-up.

Casey was unhappy that he wasn't the same person he was one year ago. He was living in fear, always wondering if the next phone call or the next person he met, or his parents met, would lead the Shorewood police to him and that he would have to break down and tell the whole story, a story he had already lied about. Was he afraid of being arrested for covering up for Bobby? He didn't think so. Was he afraid that he would be forced to rat on one of his best friends? Yes. It was simple to cover up something like stealing tomatoes, but murder was something else. Was he afraid of what his family would think of him if they found out? Yes. Or was it his father's honesty hanging over his head? That, too. He was taught to tell the truth and he was letting his father down. Who knows what Colby and Pritchard were feeling and how it affected their lives?

Lexie finally broke the silence. "Do you realize that these two guys planned the whole thing in your house?"

"They'll have to dig up the library."

Casey started thinking ahead and it worried him that he might be thrust into a limelight he hadn't bargained for.

"So? What's wrong with that?"

"The whole town will be torn apart. Don't you see?"

Casey felt guilty again. He was trying to convince Lexie that it would be all right to keep the matter quiet.

"Are you saying we shouldn't tell anyone about this?"

"I know we have to tell someone."

"Then what's the problem?"

"Why can't we just leave Ann Robertson where she is?"

"I don't believe this. First, you looked like you wanted to solve the mystery and now that you have, you want to forget about it?"

"Not really. I know. You're right."

Casey did not want to reveal his concern about the attention that would be drawn to both of them.

"Eeeeyooo!" cried Lexie. "We were right next to her. We may have stepped on her at the library."

Casey heaved a sigh of relief that Lexie changed the subject.

"Here's another strange part. He says he left some gold coins somewhere," said Casey. "Some coins? He said five hundred. That's a lot."

"What do you think happened to them?"

"He left them to his relatives. They must have gotten them."

"I guess you're right "

"What? What are you thinking now?"

"Nothing." Casey's tone of voice dropped to a mumble.

"Do you think the coins are out there somewhere waiting for us to find them?"

"Look at the code? Do you think any of his heirs figured it out?"

"It looks pretty hard to me."

"What if no one solved it?"

"I suppose the coins would still be out there somewhere."

"And if we solve the code?"

"Maybe we'd get to keep them?"

"I think we'd get at least some of them as a reward, don't you think?"

"Wow, what an imagination you've got."

"Well?"

"Well, what?"

"Suppose the coins are out there."

"That's too deep for me. You're beginning to give me the creeps. Look, we have to figure out what to do with the letter."

"You're right, as usual, but I'm going to copy the code anyway. We can work on it together while everyone else is digging up the library."

Casey and Lexie pulled out two large crates to sit on.

"My father will know what to do. He knows the town. He's so honest I'm sure he'll give the whole thing away."

It was his father's honesty, at least partly, that kept Casey from talking about Billy. He knew that if he talked to his father about what Bobby told him his father would tell the police and his promise to Bobby would be broken. How could he ever explain to his father that he knew that Bobby was with Billy that night and that he lied to him about it? If they thought Billy had been murdered, and by Rosie Germano, someone his father knew very well, it would blow the lid on everything. Now he was faced with another problem. It would be easy to tell about the letter, but Casey was afraid of all the attention it would draw to him. He had successfully kept everyone away for the past four months. If people got too close, someone, like a reporter, might connect him with the Shorewood case; he might blurt out Bobby's secret, that his own brother left him to die. Casey even made up his mind that the same reporters would cover this case. His father was a former classmate of Police Chief John Fallon. That made it even worse.

"I can't wait to see Dorothy Moorehead's face when she finds out her library will be dug up," said Lexie.

Now, Lexie was involved. If he was alone, he would have been tempted to forget the whole thing. In fact, it was only because he wanted to talk to Lexie, using the news item as an excuse, that got him here in the first place. This was not turning out well. It was one thing to solve a mystery, another to dig up a body in the library.

"We really have to think about this," said Casey.

"My father graduated with your father, maybe the two of them will come up with something."

"We're going to be famous and, maybe, rich if we find the coins," said Casey. "It's only going to cause a lot of trouble."

"Are you trying to tell me you want to hide this?"

"No, not really, but I think we ought to be careful."

"Don't mind me, I go off the deep end and exaggerate a lot."

The two sat silently for a few moments. Casey was now concerned that if he tried to hide this new event Lexie would get hurt or even murdered. It was too late to do anything else. They had to tell someone about it, but who and how?

"I think we should tell our parents, get them together," said Lexie.

"You're right." Casey was convinced, but the downcast look on his face spoke volumes about how he really felt. He did not want to add another cover-up to what he had already. If both parents knew, they might come up with a better decision and if they broke the story it might divert most of the attention away from him.

"Don't look so sad. It's not the end of the world is it?"

Casey decided not to answer that. He knew what the answer was. It was, in fact, the end of the world as he knew it. He would have to step into the spotlight whether he liked it or not.

"OK, but only if they're together when we tell them," said Casey.

Having both families together, Casey thought, might help him with the many questions that would be asked.

"Do you think you can get your mother and father to come here tomorrow?" asked Casey. "My parents won't be home until really late tonight."

"By the way, when I talked with my father the other night he said that he might have gone to school with your father. I didn't want to mention it, but, he said to ask your father if he remembers Goofy Wentworth."

"Goofy? Goofy Wentworth?"

"Something about the way he played basketball."

"He'll really be goofy when he hears about what we found?" Casey really didn't mean what he said to be funny, but he was glad that it came out that way. He wasn't sure why he let his guard down. He couldn't remember the last time he cracked a joke.

"Bad joke." Lexie smiled. "We'll have to tell them, but tomorrow I'm going away with my parents for the day. It'll have to be tomorrow night. We shouldn't wait that long, but I don't think we have any choice, do you?"

Casey thought for a moment. "No, I guess you're right. I'll tell my father that your father is coming over tomorrow night to talk about something. They know each other from high school, so it shouldn't be a problem, but make sure your mother comes, too."

"Eight o'clock will be about right, but I'll wait until five o'clock to tell him."

"OK," said Casey. "We'll explain how we got started with this thing and then show them the letter."

"What do we do with it now?"

"I want to copy the code. I'll make you a copy, too."

Casey found a pencil and a piece of scrap paper and copied the code twice, then tore off one for Lexie.

"I'll put the letter back where we found it. That way they'll believe us."

"OK, but do it now. It makes me nervous."

"On second thought, you'd better do it. I can't reach that high."

Casey and Lexie were on the brink of collapse. They shook from the excitement. Lexie returned the letter to the box, put the box back in the hole and replaced the stone.

"I need a drink," said Casey.

"What have you got?" said Lexie, "I only drink straight whiskey. Only kidding."

"Milk is the strongest I drink. C'mon upstairs. We've got cookies, too."

"Milk and cookies? At a time like this? What a treat."

"Sure, why not?"

"The rumors are all wrong. You're not such a grouch. Here you are offering me milk and cookies. People think you're mad because you're on drugs or something."

"Great. I try to mind my own business and now I'm a druggie."

They tripped over each other on the way upstairs to the kitchen. Casey went to the refrigerator and took out a bottle of milk. As Casey poured the milk, he missed Lexie's glass. Then he tipped over his own glass reaching for a cloth.

"Take it easy," said Lexie, "you might wreck the whole house."

Later, he found out that the cloth he used to wipe up the milk was a blouse Kathy had put out to be ironed.

"I need to finish fixing my bike. Want to watch?"

"Sure, I've got nothing better to do. We just solved a mystery that's been around for a hundred years and we might even end up being millionaires. The least we can do is fix your bike."

They returned to the cellar and Casey replaced the twisted wheel.

"There, that's done. What do you want to do now?" asked Casey.

"Nothing much, but I'd like to get out of here. Let's go to the mall."

They could kill some of the time at the Malt Shop in Elm Grove Harbor. It was much too cold to go for a long bicycle ride. They had to keep the secret bottled up for the next thirty hours and Casey appreciated the fact that Lexie wanted to stay with him. Lexie did most of the talking as they rode to the mall.

"Have you ever been to San Francisco?" asked Lexie.

"I've been to New Hampshire. Other than that I haven't even been out of the state. I've been out with my father on his boat, but I don't think that counts."

"I liked San Francisco, but I'm beginning to like it here, too."

"I think when I get out of school I'd like to take a trip, you know, hitchhike around the country, see things, get away from here for a while."

Casey didn't mean to blurt out the last part of his plan. Getting away was the real reason he would leave. He wanted to run, right now.

"I'd like to go to Europe some day. My mother studied in Paris."

"I'll probably end up working on my father's boat."

"You don't have to do that if you really don't want to."

"I know."

Casey bought a pad of paper and two pens at the Harbor Pharmacy. He and Lexie sat for two hours at The Harbor Malt Shop trying to break the code.

"I've never seen anything like this before," said Lexie.

"I've seen codes before. Puzzle books have them."

"I don't think Oliver Colby used a puzzle book, do you?"

Casey wrote the numbers in numerical order, 1-5-12-13-14-15-19-19-21.

"What if the numbers match letters in the alphabet?" asked Casey.

"What do you mean?"

"Suppose number one stands for the letter A."

"Then what have you got?"

Casey wrote the letters under the numbers, A-E-L-M-N-O-S-S-U.

"That makes a lot of sense to me," said Lexie. She spoke with a tone that would make one believe she was super-intelligent. Casey looked at her and smiled.

"I don't think we're going to solve this today," said Casey. "What do you think, now? Did anyone solve it?"

"Who knows? It's really hard. I can't figure it out."

"We'll just have to keep trying."

"Is your father's boat at the dock? I'd like to see it."

"He won't be there."

They rode their bikes to the pier where Casey's father's boat was docked. The tide was low. The boat was several feet below them.

"It's locked up," said Casey.

"That's OK. I didn't want to go on it. It's a great boat. You went out on it last summer?"

"For a couple of weeks before school."

A brisk, cold breeze blew in from the harbor entrance, but it did not stop Casey and Lexie from sitting on a bench at the end of the pier. They filled the time with their hopes and aspirations, their likes and dislikes, and talking about people, in general, particularly the kind of people they trusted or distrusted.

"My friends in The Sandbox Gang were really great. We spent a lot of time together."

Casey was reluctant to share what happened last summer. He became confused after Billy died. What happened to the loyalty? All of his friends bailed out on each other.

"They sound like nice kids," said Lexie. "I only had one really good friend in San Francisco and she moved away last Spring. I knew her since fifth grade. That's one of the reasons I didn't mind moving so much. There wasn't anyone else I was close to."

When the bells at St. Mary's Church rang six times, they headed for home. Neither of them said a word. The western sky was bright red and the taller trees made black silhouettes against the sky. Most of the stores were closing and traffic was thinning out along Main Street. The air was crisp and cold. At Salt Marsh Bridge, Casey and Lexie stopped.

"Thanks for coming over," said Casey. "Didn't you have something better to do?"

"Are you kidding? I don't have any friends and the only person I meet in Elm Grove solves a one hundred-year-old mystery. Of course, I had something better to do. I had a date with Elvis Presley, but I turned him down."

"Well, thanks anyway. I don't either. Have any friends, that is, until I met you."

"I'll see you tomorrow," said Casey.

Lexie nodded

Casey watched Lexie disappear at the curve in Sandy Point Road. When he arrived at his house, he noticed that a light was on in the house. The two street lamps on The Causeway had come on, but they were too far apart to provide much light near Casey's house. The boat yard was deserted. Over the boatyard, the western sky was an eerie purple color. The setting sun was hidden in the heavy overcast.

He opened the bulkhead door, but, as he dragged his bicycle to the inner cellar door, he realized that the inner door was ajar. He stepped into the darkness of the cellar and waved his hand over the tool bench until he caught a piece of string connected to a single light bulb dangling from a wire. He pulled and the light came on. He noticed that the cellar was freezing cold. As he rolled his bike into the cellar, his foot struck a solid object. He looked down and was horrified at what he saw. It was the stone, the one he had replaced to cover the tin box. The light bulb swung like a pendulum, back and forth, creating eerie shadows throughout the cellar. The sight of the gaping hole in the wall sent chills up and down Casey's spine. He grabbed a large paint can and dragged it to the wall. Standing on it, he could see into the hole.

"Now the box is gone. What next?"

Painfully, Casey reached into the hole, pulled out a crumpled piece of paper and held it up to the light. The words, Tell and you die, were scribbled on a piece of wrinkled notebook paper.

"Oh no, now what am I going to do?" Casey tried desperately to calm himself down. "I've got to call Lexie. She might be in trouble, too."

Upstairs, a single living room light was on. Ordinarily, there was a cozy and warm atmosphere in the house, but the house was chilly since no one had been home during the day to turn up the thermostat. His mother and father were still away at the wedding. Kathy left a note for him saying that she was going to stay overnight with a friend.

Casey was more aware of the gloomy shadows in the adjoining dining room and kitchen. After plugging in the window lights, Casey turned on the first lamp he could find, then another and another until every light in the house was on. As soon as he touched the thermostat, he heard the sound of the oil burner in the cellar. When he felt the hot air from the heating vents, he removed his jacket.

Casey picked up the telephone and called Lexie. "Hello?"

"Lexie?"

"What do you want?" She spoke curtly.

"Lexie, it's Casey."

"Casey. Sorry. I thought you were someone else. Some salesman keeps calling."

"You aren't going to believe this. The box is gone," Casey said.

"What? How did that happen?"

"Someone broke into the cellar and took it."

"Now what are we going to do?"

"I thought you might know. That isn't the half of it. Whoever took it left a note threatening to kill me if I tell." Casey tried to sound calm, but his voice cracked and his hands began to shake. "I'll have to tell my father tonight. This thing is getting out of hand. My parents probably won't be home until midnight and Kathy is staying overnight somewhere. Are you OK? Are your parents home?"

"I'm fine. Let me know what you want me to do. Take it easy and keep your house locked. Call me as soon as you tell him."

Casey took Lexie's advice and checked all the doors in the house making sure they were all locked. He poured himself a glass of milk, grabbed a bag of potato chips and went up to his room. He took out a pencil and paper and jotted down what he could remember about the letter. Then he looked at the scribbled attempts to break the code on the note pad and put them aside. He was too tired to think any more. He would wait for his parents and tell them as soon as they got home. Minutes later, Casey, fully dressed, drifted off to sleep. The next thing he knew it was Sunday morning.

7

Casey and Lexie Tell All

*C*asey awoke on Sunday morning as bright rays of the sun streamed through his bedroom window. He glanced at his clock through hazy eyes. It was seven thirty-five. The bad taste in his mouth reminded him that he hadn't brushed his teeth since yesterday morning. The dull ache in his ribs made him feel nauseated. He went to the bathroom, splashed cold water on his face, brushed his teeth and halfheartedly combed his hair. He paused and stared into the mirror as if he was searching for a way to get out of what he was about to do. Casey knew that, after this morning, after he told his parents the fantastic tale about Anne Robertson, his life would change again and he was sure it would not be for the better.

The house was silent, but the aroma of freshly brewed coffee was a sign that his father was up and about. No one else but his father would be up this early on Sunday morning. For years Ed Miller worked from the early morning hours until sundown. In Spring and Summer he spent ten days at a time far out at sea. At this time of year, from late November through mid-February, except for two weeks at the end of January he only went out for short daily trips. Today, like every Sunday morning, when his father was at home, as long as Casey could remember, his father would get up at least two hours before anyone else in the family. As usual, he would be casually dressed in his gray and green flannel shirt with faded blue Levi's and dark brown heavy wool socks. He had already made a fresh pot of coffee for the rest of the family when they arose. He was settled comfortably in his favorite chair, a dark brown leather lounge chair that tilted back. The chair was tilted as far back as it would go and his father looked like an astronaut waiting for liftoff, his stocking feet higher than his head. A steamy cup of hot, black coffee sat on the table next to his chair and beside that was the faded gray baseball cap he frequently wore, seemingly at the ready in case he had to leave the house. Parts of the Sunday paper were strewn around his chair, discarded after his father read them. Casey swore that his father read every word of the Sunday paper, including the classified ads.

Ed Miller was tall and muscular, a man with the build that would match a well-seasoned, well-tanned athlete. At six feet three inches tall he was five inches taller than Casey. His face was the color of the leather chair he was sitting in. He had a three-inch scar on his face that he got when he was teenager working on his father's fishing boat. He was standing in the wrong place when a cable snapped and slapped him in the face. His hair was cut short with a crew cut. His receding hair line was a lighter tan than his face, because he wore a baseball cap most of the time no matter where he was, at sea or on shore. His hands were coarse and deeply tanned while his arms were much lighter in color, because he wore long-sleeved shirts to protect himself from the harsh sun at sea. Both of his hands were swollen from cuts and bruises, sprains and breaks suffered at the hands of cantankerous lobster traps, tangled fishing lines and from crawling in and out of the engine compartment of all the fishing vessels he worked on since he was fourteen years old.

Despite the toughness of his appearance, Ed was a patient, quiet man, not easily ruffled, a private man who had no desire to socialize with people outside a one-mile limit from the fish pier. He had a peaceful self-reliance learned from years of experience facing the many challenges put to him by a restless and unpredictable ocean in all kinds of weather. He was well trained by the best fishermen on the East coast, including three generations of fishermen in his own family.

Casey's mother, on the other hand, was of a different makeup, more outgoing, emotional and, although she leaned toward a cautious side when dealing with her children, she was not overprotective. She was more accustomed to dealing with the public having worked in doctors' offices since graduating from high school. Julie Miller enjoyed meeting people from all walks of life and dealt with rich people or poor, famous or not, with the same level of respect. She dressed casually and simply, but always aware of what was fashionable.

"Dad, we've got to talk," said Casey.

Without looking up from his newspaper, apparently trying to finish an article he was reading, Casey's father grunted a response then looked up. "What happened to you? You look like death warmed over. Did you sleep in your clothes?"

"Maybe Mom ought to hear this, too,"

"Your mother is still asleep. What's going on?"

"Did Mom tell you about the ring?" Casey hoped he hadn't revealed his mother's secret.

"She did, last night." Mr. Miller answered, "What's this about?"

"It belonged to Jonathan Pritchard and he gave it to Anne Robertson, a girl who disappeared a long time ago," Casey said. "That's what the AR to JMP is all about."

"What are you talking about? Who's Anne Robertson?"

"Inside Mom's ring, it says AR to JMP."

"What about it? Most old rings have something on them."

"This one is special, Dad. Lexie and I found out whose initials they are."

"Lexie? Who's Lexie?"

"Sorry, Dad, she's a girl I met at school."

"What's she got to do with the ring?"

"Can we wake Mom up?"

"We were out late last night. She's tired. What's this all about?"

"There's a plaque at the high school for a girl named Anne Robertson."

"Oh, that Anne Robertson. How do you know about that?"

"It's a long story. Can't we wake Mom up?" Then Casey saw his mother coming down the stairs dressed in a pink bathrobe.

"You'd better come and hear this, Julie," said Mr. Miller.

"Let me get my coffee."

"Bring in the pot. I'll have a refill."

Mrs. Miller went to the kitchen and returned with a steaming pot of coffee and a mug. "Now, what's wrong?" she asked as she filled Mr. Miller's cup. She remained standing while Casey talked.

Casey thought to himself, "Why is it that mothers always ask what's wrong when you want to talk about something? In this case, she's right. Something is wrong."

"Do you remember a plaque with a girl named Ann Robertson's name on it at the high school?" asked Mr. Miller

"Yes, I remember. In fact, one of my teachers spent a whole period talking about it. He was fascinated by old unsolved mysteries. He liked that one because it started a feud between three families. The plaque used to be in the old high school. The Robertson family lived up on Sandy Point Road."

"Casey says the ring you bought belonged to the missing Robertson girl."

"How do you know that?" asked Mrs. Miller.

Before she could go on, Casey interrupted her. "I found an old newspaper article in my new, locker. It isn't really a locker, it's a closet. Anyway, it was about Anne Robertson disappearing. It happened in 1898. Lexie Wentworth, a friend I met in school, she has the closet next to mine, and I went up to the high school to see the plaque that the town put up in her memory. Then we went to the library and saw her picture in her old yearbook."

"What's so unusual about that?" Mr. Miller asked.

"Lexie and I went back to the library that same night. The yearbook was missing, so we looked up the old newspapers on the microfiche. We saw all the articles written about Anne."

"And?" Mrs. Miller asked.

"On the way home someone tried to run me over at Salt Marsh Bridge."

"When did that happen?" asked Mr. Miller.

"Last Thursday night."

"Why didn't you tell us? Were you hurt?" Mrs. Miller walked over to Casey and put her hand on his forehead.

"It's just a bruise on my ribs, Mom, my head is OK. I didn't want you to get upset. My bike got the worst of it. The front wheel was totaled. That's not the whole story. The good part is coming."

Mr. Miller adjusted his chair to an upright position. Mrs. Miller sat on the couch nearby. Casey continued with his story.

"Lexie came over yesterday morning to see my bike and while I was working on it she poked around at a loose stone in the cellar wall. I pulled it out and found an old tin box in the hole. I opened the box and found a letter written by someone named Oliver Colby. I know we should have told you about it yesterday, but you weren't at home."

"It might be valuable. You know this is the old Colby house," said Mrs. Miller.

"Never mind that now," said Mr. Miller, "get on with it."

"He said that Jason Pritchard's horse hit Anne and she died. He was driving home in a rainstorm and didn't see Anne. Anyway, Oliver Colby said that he and Jason buried Anne's body in the library cellar."

Casey paused to see the reaction from his parents. Neither of his parents said a word. They looked at each other, then looked at Casey. He continued.

"The letter was written in 1898."

For some reason, Casey withheld the part about the gold coins and the code.

"Where's the letter?" Mrs. Miller asked.

"Lexie and I were going to break the news to you tonight. Lexie was going to have her father come over here to help decide what to do. So, we put the letter back in the box and put the box back in the hole. Then we went to the Harbor."

"So?" Mr. Miller asked.

"So, somebody got into our cellar and stole the box."

"You mean someone broke into our cellar and you didn't tell us about it?" The tone of Mr. Miller's voice suggested that he was getting more than just impatient. He rose from his chair and faced Casey with an accusatory manner.

"I am telling you," said Casey testily. "You were away until late last night and I was so tired I fell asleep."

"How would anyone know about the letter? Did you tell anyone else?" Mr. Miller spoke so quickly Casey had no chance to answer. Casey could tell that his father was getting more upset, a side he rarely saw, even with some of the antics of The Sandbox Gang, but someone had invaded his turf, broke into his house and that was entirely different. "Show me where you found it."

Casey wasn't sure whether his father and mother believed him. It was a strange story and he had no evidence at all to show them. It would have been much easier if he left well enough alone and ignored the news item. He could not understand how all the other people who owned the house never found the letter. Now, with the letter stolen, it would be hard for Casey and Lexie to convince anyone that they had solved the mystery of Anne's disappearance. Who would believe two teenagers? Would they dig up the library just because two teenagers claimed that someone was buried there?

"We have to do something, but what?" Casey muttered to himself as he led the way to the cellar. On the way, he told his father and mother that Lexie and he had no idea who knew about the letter. In the cellar, Casey pointed to the hole in the wall and the stone on the cellar floor. At that point, Casey saw Kathy coming down the cellar stairs.

"What's going on?" she asked.

Casey gave her a brief summary.

"You sure know how to treat a girl on a date," said Kathy.

"Never mind that," said Mr. Miller.

"The stone is over there." Casey pointed to it.

"That's funny," said Mr. Miller, "I was about to put some cement on that stone. I noticed it was loose, but didn't touch it. It's a good thing I didn't. I might have just sealed it with cement and not taken the stone out. We might never have found out about Anne."

"What should we do now? If the story gets out, the whole town will freak out," said Casey.

"Let's think about this for a minute. You're right. The town will come apart at the seams. We'd better get Lexie's parents over here. She may be in danger, too. Whatever we do we should decide together. Kathy, don't breathe a word to your friends until we get this straightened out."

Casey heaved a sigh of relief. His parents weren't going to call the police, at least not for a while.

Kathy nodded, but Casey knew how hard it would be for her to keep this kind of secret. Her friends would love it.

Casey telephoned Lexie and hoped she hadn't left yet.

"Lexie? Oh, man, am I glad you're still there. Can you and your parents come right over? I told my father and he thinks we ought to get together right away."

"Leave it to me, I'll get them there."

In less than an hour, Lexie and her father and mother, Bob and Bonnie Wentworth, were at the door.

"Goofy Wentworth. I haven't seen you since high school. Last time I heard, you were in California. How have you been?" asked Mr. Miller.

"Just great, Ed. This is my wife, Bonnie, this is Ed Miller and his wife, Julie. Gosh, you both haven't changed a bit."

"Don't give me that sales talk. I knew you in high school."

Casey whispered to Lexie, "Do they know?"

"Not all of it. I thought it would be better if they all heard it together," said Lexie.

"I haven't told them about the coins or the code."

"This ought to be fun."

When they finished reacquainting themselves, the group sat in the living room. Mrs. Miller brought a pot of coffee and a coffee cake, the family's usual Sunday morning fare. Casey repeated the story for the group. He omitted the part about the coins. Mr. Miller got up and started pacing the floor. Casey never realized his father could be so upset.

"I forgot to tell you something else," Casey said.

"There's more?" asked Mr. Miller.

"The person who broke in left this note." Casey reached into his pocket and handed his father the death threat note. Mr. Miller read it and fell into his chair. He passed it to his wife. All she could say was, "Oh, my." She gave it to Mrs. Wentworth and she passed it to Mr. Wentworth. All were speechless.

"Somebody wants to keep this quiet. We'd better call John Fallon," Mr. Miller said. "Unless you've got a better idea," he asked Mr. and Mrs. Wentworth.

"That sounds good to me, but I'm worried about the death threat," said Mr. Wentworth. "I just hope things don't get out of hand. Once the police know about this they have to act. We can't take a chance on that note being a bluff. If the police do anything, there could be trouble. Do you think you can get Chief Fallon to come here? He should be at home. You never know who'll be at the station."

"It'll be better if we break the news away from the station, don't you think?" asked Mrs. Wentworth.

"Are we all agreed?"

All but Casey nodded agreement.

Casey and Lexie listened carefully to his father calling Chief John Fallon. There was nothing anyone could do until Chief Fallon made a decision.

"John, you'd better get over here right away. No, it can't wait. No, I can't tell you on the phone, especially at the station. Believe me, it's important." Mr. Miller put the phone down and said, "He'll be here in an hour."

While they waited Casey and Lexie sat at the Miller's dining room table while their parents had their own discussion in the living room.

"What's the deal about the coins?" whispered Lexie.

"If we tell we might not get the reward if there is one, besides, there might not be any after all."

"Maybe, but how do we find out if there are any?"

"I guess we'll have to break the code."

Casey noticed that Lexie used the word "we" when she spoke. He smiled at her and said, "You aren't interested in that, are you?"

"Of course, I am, we're going to split the reward, aren't we?"

"Sure."

The two were silent for a moment, each trying to think of another topic to talk about.

"What are you going to be when you grow up?" asked Lexie.

"What made you think of that?"

"I don't know. I'm just curious. That news item, for instance. I wouldn't have done a thing with it. You could have thrown it away."

"That's no big deal."

"What about the ring? If you hadn't made the connection, we wouldn't be in this mess."

"I know and I'm sorry I got you into it."

"Are you kidding? I've never had this much fun. I thought this only happened in the movies. Why did you ask me about all this stuff?"

"Why did you come along with me?"

"I asked you first."

"Casey and Lexie. Would you come in here?" It was Casey's mother.

"Saved again. I'll find out yet," said Lexie.

Casey answered more questions from the parents as they all nervously waited for Chief Fallon to arrive. Who had Casey and Lexie come in contact with? Where had they been? Did Casey get the license number of the car? Did he recognize the car? Did they notice anyone suspicious wherever they were? All Casey and Lexie could remember was Jake Colby and Dorothy Moorhead. Casey was getting more nervous. He didn't like the idea that he might be questioned by the Chief of Police. He had enough in Shorewood. This time he would have to face Chief John Fallon, a friend of both families. They were Interrupted by a loud pounding on the front door.

Casey recognized Chief Fallon right away. In a small town like Elm Grove it was a common sight to see the popular, genial giant driving around the town or visiting the townspeople at the Harbor Coffee Shop. He got a great deal of satisfaction out of people calling him Chief. Except for a stint in the Vietnam War, he was a lifelong, well-respected resident of Elm Grove. He towered over most of the people he met with an ego to match. Casey thought he had to be at least six feet five inches tall and with his bright red hunting jacket and dark blue knit cap he looked like a poster of Paul Bunyan standing on the front porch. With his looks and stature he could very well be the subject of a recruitment poster for the Marines, the branch of service he served in during a stint in the Vietnam War.

After graduating from Elm Grove High School, The Chief attended junior college, worked at odd jobs and served two years in Vietnam. When he got out of the service, he joined the Elm Grove police force. While Ed and Julie were in Shorewood, John Falcon scored exceptionally high on the police exam, accumulated an outstanding record as a patrol-man and detective and took additional advanced professional courses. Finally, he achieved his lifelong dream when he was appointed Chief of Police. A cold draft of air accompanied him as he stepped into the kitchen.

"Hello, everybody," said Chief Fallon as he removed his coat and hat. He ran his fingers through his closely-cut, graying black hair.

No one spoke. Each waited for the other to open the conversation about Anne Robertson.

"It must be pretty serious to get me out on Sunday morning. What's going on?"

Mrs. Miller broke the silence. "Let's go into the living room."

Mrs. Miller served everyone a mug of coffee, then Casey repeated the details of the adventure. He concentrated on the news item, the plaque, the rings, the stolen box with the letter and the death threat, but still he remained silent about the coins. When he finished, he decided to test the waters to see if he could learn more about what would happen if the coins were found.

"Chief Fallon, what happens if someone finds a treasure around here?" asked Casey.

"Why? Have you got one?"

"No, I just want to know."

"Do you mean sunken treasure?"

"No," replied Lexie. "You know. Stuff in an attic or something."

"I suppose it gets turned over to the state or the federal government depending on where it's found and what the treasure is. I'm not sure."

"Then what?"

"Most likely they would try to find out who owned it and it would go to that person's estate, otherwise, I assume it would go to a museum. Again, it depends on what the treasure is and if it is authentic. An expert has to look at it to put a value on it."

"What do the finders get?"

"I suppose there could be a reward, but don't quote me on that and I wouldn't count on the government to issue one."

Casey changed the subject. He noticed that Lexie had a strange look on her face, as if she was expecting Casey to talk more about the coins.

"What do you think will happen to the town when the news gets out?" asked Mrs. Miller.

"At this time of year good stories are scarce, especially in a small town like Elm Grove. This ought to attract an army of journalists and photographers. It could get ugly."

"We could have kept this quiet," said Lexie.

Casey interrupted her before she could go on and mention the coins.

"But, Lexie and I would have felt guilty if we covered this up, besides, things started getting out of hand with the box stolen."

When Casey glanced at Lexie, Lexie held up her hands with a quizzical look on her face as if to say 'what about the coins?' and 'what about the death threat.' Casey returned her look and gestured with his hands for her to keep quiet.

"No matter what happens, you did the right thing," said The Chief.

Casey hoped The Chief would go slow with this and not get him more involved than he was already. By the look on The Chief's face, Casey could tell he was more than just casually concerned.

"Show me where you found the box," said the Chief.

The group went to the cellar where Casey and Lexie repeated their story.

The Chief looked at the hole in the wall from every possible angle. Actually, he had to duck his head to walk around in the cellar.

"I'm afraid I'll have to seal off the cellar for a while. I need to get someone in here to look for clues, fingerprints, that sort of thing, but it might be several days. Don't upset anything down here."

"I found the stone over here, the one I put back. I haven't moved it," said Casey.

"Good. Leave it there and I'll make a note of it. So, he came through the bulkhead door over here?"

"Right," said Casey. He was beginning to feel like he was part of a detective squad, but, at the same time he knew he would have to keep his distance for fear that the case in Shorewood would come up.

The Chief stepped through the cellar door and pushed open the bulkhead. He wrote on a note pad and then said, "Let's go back upstairs." On the way up, he asked, "Isn't this the old Colby House, Ed?"

"That's right. It's on the original deed," Ed replied.

"And there's a brass plate at the front door with the name on it," said Kathy.

They all watched as Ed rummaged through a set of papers in the old desk that occupied a corner of the living room. "Here, it says that it was built by Oliver Colby in 1894. When Oliver died in 1908, the deed changed to his son, Andrew. The house was sold to a George and Alice Cooper in 1947. They sold it to Harry and Matilda Johnson in 1968. When they died, they left it to the Historical Society to do with as they pleased. We bought it from the Society.".

"Is Jake Colby related to Oliver?" asked Casey.

"Yes, he was Olive's grandson, Andrew's son. His father's name was Harold," said the Chief, "why do you ask?"

"He works at the library. He saw us looking at the microfiche. Jake might have been the one who took the yearbook, too."

"What about the yearbook? Is there something else you haven't told us?" asked Mr. Miller.

"When we went to the library the first time we found Anne's picture," said Casey. "We went back to the library to see if we could find out who JMP was on the ring I found. We thought we would find out who he was in the old yearbook we saw before."

"When we went back, the yearbook was gone," said Lexie.

"Then Mom came home with another ring."

"Wait just a minute," asked Mr. Miller. "You mean the ring your mother told me about last night?"

"I bought it a few days ago," said Julie.

"There are two rings?" asked The Chief.

"Yes, I found the first one in my closet at school."

"Anne Robertson's initials are on both rings," said Casey.

"And her boyfriend, Jonathan Pritchard's, too," said Lexie.

"So that's why you got so excited," said Kathy. "I thought you'd gone crazy."

"Do you think Jake is involved in this somehow?" said the Chief.

"He was acting pretty strange at the library," said Lexie. "He gave me the creeps."

"Why didn't this house go to Jake?" asked Julie.

"As far as I know," the Chief explained, "Jake left home when he was about nineteen years old. He went out west to make his fortune and did some time in the Army, too. While he was away, his father died. His mother became very ill and had to sell the house. She died in a nursing home before Jake got back. As far as I know, Jake is the only survivor of the whole Colby clan."

"Then Jake must be the one who knew about the letter," said Casey. "And he must be the one who tried to run me over."

"Run you over? What are you talking about?" asked Mrs. Miller.

"On the way home from the library someone ran me off the road."

"Are you hurt?" asked his father.

"Just some bruised ribs. I'm OK."

"Why didn't you tell us," asked his mother.

"You'd have me up in South Shore Hospital by now."

"You didn't just punch him in the ribs, did you, Lexie?" asked Kathy. Lexie smiled.

"This is no joke," said Casey's father. "If it was Jake, he means business."

The group went silent. No one spoke for several minutes. They all tried to absorb everything that was said and to figure out what to do next.

Casey still did not know why he held back about the coins, but he decided he would not tell about them until later. If Jake Colby was the only survivor and did not get back in time for the sale of the house, he may not have gotten the coins. It must have been Jake who stole the box. Now, he has the letter and, by now, he knows about the existence of the coins. But, why would he leave a death threat?

Bob Wentworth broke the silence. "When you read your deed it made me think about our house. There was a Pritchard family that owned it many years ago, but I never made a connection until now. The Robertson house and the Pritchard house are in a book we have about historical homes. The Pritchards built ours."

"Do you think there's another letter hidden in our house?" asked Lexie.

Chief Fallon responded. "That's unlikely, but you could look. I don't have any evidence to do anything. I can order a search of the library, but, what if Anne Robertson isn't buried there?"

"Christmas time isn't the best time to go digging up the library," said Mr. Wentworth.

"You're right about that," said Mrs. Miller.

"I can tell you right now that won't happen," said The Chief. "It will be bad enough when we do it, but there's no sense in spoiling Christmas. The media will go crazy here. Even if there is someone buried there, it may take months to identify the remains. I need some evidence to connect Pritchard and Colby and it looks like the letter is the only piece of evidence. Casey is right. The whole town will come apart at the seams and without the letter I'd be a laughing stock for digging up the library if nothing is there. You've got to admit, this doesn't sound like the sanest story ever told."

"Do you mean you're not going to do anything?" asked Lexie.

"Not until after Christmas, anyway," replied The Chief. I just need more than what we've got to take any drastic steps and digging up the library is a drastic step."

Casey saw the worried look on the Chief's face and he knew that if the Chief didn't act, he might have a hard time explaining why. Then Casey realized that if the Wentworths didn't find a letter there would be no evidence at all. *What will Jake do when he hears that the police are going to search the library? Will he kill me? At least The Chief is going to wait for a while.*

Casey motioned to Lexie to go outside with him through the front door.

"Why didn't you tell them about the coins?" asked Lexie.

"I don't know. I guess I didn't want to complicate things more than they are already. Are you going to tell your mother and father?"

"No, unless you want me to."

"Let's wait and see what happens after Christmas."

"It's all right with me."

"Come in, Casey. You'll catch cold without a coat on." It was Casey's mother at the front door. The Wentworths and The Chief were on the way out.

"See you later, Lexie. Goodbye, Mr. and Mrs. Wentworth," said Casey. "Hope you find another letter."

Then, he listened intently to Chief Fallon instructing his father and mother, Kathy and him on what to do to protect themselves. There was no telling what might happen next.

"I'll call you tomorrow from home," said The Chief. "I need to get things in order to start a legal search. I want to do it quietly, get everything done before I make any announcement. If I call from the office, someone might not understand what's going on. I'll have to contact the county coroner, too. He should be at the library when we go in. I want him to supervise the job. If we find anything, he'll have to take charge of the remains. It won't be a simple matter. Keeping the press on a leash won't be easy either. In the meantime, I'll assign a man to keep an eye on your house, but I won't tell him anything except that we suspect a prowler is in the area. The fewer people who know about this and the little they know the better it will be for now."

After everyone left, Casey's mother locked the front door. Casey went up to his room until noon, then went for a walk on the beach by himself. He needed the cold, clear air and the solitude of the beach to clear his head. There was a lot to deal with. When he got back to his house, he got a message from Lexie. Her mother was driving Lexie to school on Monday morning. She would pick him up at seven-thirty. He spent the rest of the day in his room. By nightfall he had a plan.

8

A Home Visit

When Casey awoke on Monday morning, he was still tired. He could hardly to keep his eyes open as he got ready for school and ate his breakfast. Instead of waiting at home for Lexie and her mother, he decided to walk toward Salt Marsh Bridge. He was halfway there when the Wentworth family's car approached.

"Hi, Casey," said Lexie.

Casey grunted an answer and got into the back seat behind Mrs. Wentworth.

"I guess you aren't talking to me today," said Lexie.

Casey remained silent until they got to school. He went off by himself to his classes. Lexie shrugged her shoulders and kissed her mother goodbye.

"Thanks, Mom. See you later."

"Do you want me to pick you up? It's supposed to snow, you know," asked Mrs. Wentworth.

"No. I'll see if I can touch base with Casey. Something's wrong."

Throughout the day Casey mulled over his plan. He felt certain that the person who threatened his life must be Jake Colby. Who else could it be? Would Jake carry out his threat if he knew that Casey told the police? Maybe if the Wentworths found another letter, it would give The

Chief the evidence he needed, but if they didn't the case would be lost. After school, Casey waited for Lexie and they walked home together. A light snow started falling.

"What's wrong with you?" asked Lexie. "You didn't say a word to me all day."

"I'm sorry," said Casey. "I've got a lot on my mind."

"You've got a lot on your mind? What about me? You got me into to this and you won't talk? I haven't known you for very long, but I think you owe me that much. What's eating you?"

By the time they arrived at Salt Marsh Bridge the snowfall was heavier. Casey turned to Lexie and, with a worried look on his face said, "I've got a plan, but I'm not sure you should go along with me."

"Try me."

"We've got to do something. Can you meet me at the bridge at eight tonight?"

"I guess so. What for?"

Casey was torn between waiting to tell her his plan and telling her now. He was afraid she would say yes, but more afraid that she would say no, but if she said no, he might be able to convince her if it was closer to the time when he wanted to act.

"I'll tell you when you get there. Wear warm clothes."

Casey walked away before Lexie could say anything else. He had a plan and he would not be able to carry it out without Lexie's help. He was afraid she might back out.

* · * *

Casey had to sneak out of his house to avoid telling his parents and he had to avoid the policeman who was supposed to watch his house. It was snowing hard, a wet and heavy snow. Already there were two or three inches on the ground. The snow plows would not be around to plow the road in front of his house or on Sandy Point until after midnight. Carefully, he opened the porch door and, after making sure that the police cruiser was nowhere in sight, he ran to the sea wall. A flashlight in hand, Casey jumped over the sea wall, trotted along the beach and cut back onto The Causeway to Salt Marsh Bridge. He saw someone leaning against the light pole at the bridge. It was Lexie with her coat collar pulled up over her face trying to shield herself from the falling snow and the biting wind blowing across the marsh.

"What's the flashlight for? Going somewhere?" mumbled Lexie. Her breath came out in white puffs escaping between her red knit cap and her coat collar. "This better be good to get me out on a night like this."

"We're going to Jake Colby's house," said Casey.

"I thought I heard you say Jake Colby's house?"

"Don't you remember? The Chief can't get into the case without any evidence and the letter is the only thing out there. Jake is the only one I can think of who has it. Did you find another letter?"

"No. We looked everywhere. My parents have given up."

"Then we've got to go now. Jake must have the letter we found."

"Unless he's burned it."

Before Lexie knew what he was doing, Casey started walking across the bridge toward Pritchard's Corner.

"We don't know that. He knows about the coins, too. He wouldn't burn that. It's his only claim to the coins."

"That's really smart. How did you figure that out?"

"I did a lot of thinking yesterday and today."

"You sure did and you didn't speak a word to me."

"I know and I'm sorry about that, but we've got to find out. It's the only way I can think of to dig up the evidence The Chief needs."

"He's going to dig up the library. Isn't that enough?"

"You know that's not enough. Even if they test the bones and find out how old they are, it won't mean a thing unless we have the letter to prove what really happened."

"But, why are we going to Jake Colby's house tonight?"

"I think he's the one who stole the letter. I'm sure he's the one who tried to run me over and he must have been the one who left the note. If he solves the code, he gets the coins."

"You can't be sure about that? And what if we're caught? Jake will be at home. Then, what are you going to do?"

"We're not going to get caught. I just want to see what his house is like. We'll just case the joint."

"You mean Casey the joint?"

"Very funny."

"Are you acting in a movie or what?"

"We'll play it by ear. If Jake is out, we'll go in, if not, then at least we'll know what we have to do later."

"Why are you doing this?"

"Have you got a better idea?"

"Yeah, a warm bed."

"This is important, Lexie. If we don't do something, the whole thing will be unsolved and forgotten. We may never have a chance like this again."

"Why did you pick on poor old me? Why didn't you ask one of those girls in blue and white? Look at me. Do I look like the kind of girl who needs to be walking in a snow storm talking about breaking into someone's house? That's what you mean, isn't it? You're going to break into Jake Colby's house."

"I didn't say that, but now that I think about it, I guess that's what we're going to do if we get the chance."

"But why? Why can't you leave this alone?"

"I didn't know it was going to turn out like this, but now that it has, I need your courage, your loyalty, your intelligence."

"All right, already. Enough! What do you want me to do?"

"I don't even know what I'm going to do."

"I must be crazy to go along with this."

"Just stay with me, that's all."

Lexie shrugged her shoulders, threw up her arms and followed Casey through the snow. Light from a street lamp at Pritchard's Corner cast eerie shadows over a white blanket of undisturbed snow. In the dark it was difficult to see how heavy the snow was falling, but, against the light, streaks of the wet snowfall were clearly visible. Melted snow dripped from Casey's face and the icy cold breeze reddened his cheeks.

"We'll go in from the back, up Wood Road to Oak Lane," said Casey. "Then we'll go through the cemetery to the back of Jake's house."

"Funny, I haven't been to that part of town yet."

As the pair walked up Oak Lane they could see inside some of the houses where people were watching television.

"Look at those lucky people," said Lexie. "I could be home in my room nice and warm."

Casey continued his way in silence.

"Why do I get the feeling I'm talking to myself?"

Their footsteps made deep imprints in the wet snow. Already small mounds of snow were forming on each gravestone. Stately, leafless trees stood guard throughout the cemetery. Their branches crackled in the wind. Jake's house was at the far end of the cemetery. Casey kept the light from his flashlight pointing almost straight down in front of him. There was an access road to the cemetery, but it was covered with snow. The two trudged through the grounds wending their way through the gravestones until they reached Jake's back yard. Casey turned the light into Lexie's face.

"I'm still here," she whispered. "Why, I don't know, but I'm here."

A three-foot stone wall separated Jake's yard from the cemetery grounds. Casey climbed over the wall first, but not without great effort. He had to push aside thick brush that grew wild on Jake's side of the wall. Branches had to be broken to make a path and the accumulated snow soaked Casey's jacket.

"Are you sure you want to go through with this?" whispered Lexie.

Casey didn't answer. He was too busy trying to steer his way through the brush.

"Casey? Are you there?"

"I'm over here. Come this way." He turned the flashlight in Lexie's direction and she followed it over the wall.

Once both of them were over the wall, Casey turned the flashlight off. It was still snowing and the temperature was dropping. The dampness in the air made it feel colder. The only light in the area came from a window in Jake's house approximately thirty yards from the wall. Casey and Lexie had to struggle through a heavy growth of leafless shrubs and tall uncut grass to get to the lighted window.

"This way," Casey whispered.

He crouched low. Lexie kept close to his heels, and held on tight to Casey's jacket. A ray of light from Jake's dining room window created a yellowish glow on the ground. Casey pressed himself against the wall next to the window and Lexie did the same. They heard the muffled sound of voices coming from inside the house.

"Shhhh. Don't make a sound," whispered Casey. Lexie nodded.

Together, Casey and Lexie moved under the window and carefully raised their heads. Inside, two people were arguing.

"It's Jake and Dorothy Moorehead," whispered Lexie. "I thought you said Jake would be at the library. And what's Dorothy doing in there?"

"I was sure Jake would be at work, but I have no idea what she's doing in there?"

"I don't like it. Let's get out of here," said Lexie.

"Wait a minute," said Casey, "Look, on the table. It's the tin box."

By the looks on their faces, Jake and Dorothy were not in a friendly frame of mind. A single floor lamp lit the room and in that light their grimacing faces were frightening, unlike the way they looked on the job at the library. Despite the old storm windows covering the window Casey and Lexie could hear their conversation.

"I'm not paying you one red cent more," said Jake.

"That's what you think. I've still got Jason's letter. If you don't want your family's name spread all over the place, you'll keep paying, and more. You'll be washed up in this town and they may even take away your inheritance."

Dorothy took out her handkerchief and wiped her nose.

"They can't do anything to me," said Jake. "It's over. I'm through with you. It doesn't matter anymore."

"Did you hear that? There is another letter. Dorothy has it," whispered Casey.

"I'm freezing, let's go home."

"I am, too. Just another minute and we'll go."

The dim light over Jake's dining room table revealed the clutter of years and years of accumulated newspapers, furniture, pictures and odds and ends inherited from previous generations. Amid a scattered collection of papers and letters, on the dining room table, Jake placed the tin box containing Oliver Colby's letter. He removed the letter from the box and held it up to show Dorothy.

"This is a letter Oliver Colby wrote on the night of Anne Robertson's death."

"How did you get this?" asked Dorothy.

"Those two teenagers made me get it."

"What teenagers? Oh, you mean the ones who came to look at the yearbook?"

"Right."

"They're harmless. Those kids don't know anything."

"They know everything. They found my great-grandfather's letter."

"How?"

"My great-grandfather Colby hid this letter in his house foundation. I've known for years it was there. I found out when I got hold of my grandmother's belongings. They were put in storage after she died. Old Jason was clever, too. Somehow, he knew Oliver would do something to cover himself in case something went wrong. After they buried Anne, he was so paranoid that he wrote his own letter. That's the one you have."

Lexie whispered, "I'm freezing. Let's go. We've found out what we came here for."

"No, we haven't. Now there are two letters. We have to find a way to get them."

"Didn't you hear me? I'm freezing."

Casey saw that Lexie was shivering and bothered by the cold. Reluctantly, he led the way back over the stone wall.

*   *   *

Meanwhile, inside Jake's house the conversation continued.

Dorothy said, "Jason knew Oliver well enough to know not to trust him completely. So, he figured Oliver might do something to cover himself. He went home to write his own version to guarantee Oliver's silence by blackmailing Oliver in case Oliver decided to confess. That's the letter I have. It was left to me in an old trunk. How did you know those teenagers got a hold of Oliver's letter?"

"I didn't. I was in the cellar of the library when those teenagers came in asking for the 1898 yearbook. I hid while they looked at the yearbook and heard them talk about Anne Robertson."

"I didn't pay any attention to that. People ask me to look up all kinds of things."

"I knew something was going on when they came back and looked through the microfiche records. I decided it was time to stop whatever it was they were doing."

"What do you mean? What have you done?"

"I knew there was a box in the cellar at the old Colby house, but I couldn't get to it, but when I saw them at the library I had to take a chance, so I went in and got the box. I didn't know they found it. I did-n't even know what I would find in the box. When I got to it, it had been opened, but this letter was still there. I put a scare into that Miller boy, too. I'll take care of him and he'll take care that his girl friend keeps quiet. I've got the box and everything will be just as it was. They'll never find out the real story."

"How do you know I won't tell? How do you know they haven't told already?"

"They'll never believe those teenagers."

"They'll dig up the library and find Anne's bones."

"How are they going to tell if they're Anne Robertson's bones? They won't find out a thing as long as I have the letters and those teenagers will never forget the scare I put into them."

"What do you mean, a scare? Are you crazy? What have you done?"

"I just ran the Miller boy off the road and my note should take care of the rest. Now, he knows I mean business."

"A note? You left a note? They'll trace it, I'm sure they will. What have you done? This is getting out of hand."

"What's the matter, Dorothy, getting nervous?"

"I'm stopping this, right now. Either you do the same or I'll turn this in myself."

"You have the one letter I need to shut this whole thing up and you aren't going to tell anyone. If you decide to tell, I'll use this one to save my good name and you'll face blackmail charges. I'm not paying you another cent."

"You'll be sorry, Jake. I think you're bluffing." Dorothy grabbed the box and made a dash for the door.

Before she could open it, Jake grabbed her arm? "Give me the box," he growled.

"No, I'm getting out of here. We stay the same. You'll pay or I go to the police."

"Give me the box, you fool."

"Get away from me."

"Not until I have the box."

The two grappled with each other until Jake overpowered Dorothy and grabbed the box.

"Now, get out and stay out."

"I'll be back in two days, Jake. You'll pay me then, or I go to the police."

                *   *   *

Meanwhile, Casey and Lexie stopped at the entrance to the cemetery, both bent over, breathless. Lexie leaned against a lamp post.

"Now what are you going to do? Notice I said you, not we?" asked Lexie.

"I know we have to tell our parents about this."

"I'm still freezing. I can't believe we did this."

They went on to Salt Marsh Bridge in silence.

"Go home and tell your parents. I'll tell mine," said Casey. "They may want to call Chief Fallon."

"OK, talk to you later," said Lexie as she hurried away.

Casey walked as fast he could through the deepening snow. The Causeway was invisible under a smooth blanket of drifting snow. There were no tracks in the snow and he could not see the police cruiser ahead. He pulled open the outside bulkhead door, pushed the cellar door open and scrambled up the cellar stairs. His mother heard the commotion and stood in amazement as Casey stumbled into the kitchen.

"Casey, what on earth is going on?" said his mother.

"Where's Dad? I have to tell him something."

"He's in the living room. Where have you been?"

Casey rushed into the living room still covered with wet snow. "Dad, Lexie and I just saw Jake Colby and Dorothy Moorehead talking at

Jake's house and Jake has the letter and the tin box and Dorothy has a second letter."

"Slow down," said Mr. Miller. "How do you know that?"

"Lexie and I sneaked up on them and saw them in Jake's house."

"You did what? Did they see you?" Casey's father stood up with a worried look on his face.

Casey settled down and explained more clearly where he and Lexie had been and what they saw. "What do you think, Dad?"

"I don't know what to think. What does Dorothy Moorehead have to do with this? I'd better call The Chief."

Casey stood by while his father explained the latest development to The Chief.

"What did he say, Dad?" asked Casey.

"He said to tell you not to pull a fool stunt like that again, but, it gives him something to work on. He'll get in touch with us."

The phone rang. Casey's father answered. He spoke briefly. "That was Lexie's father. Lexie told him everything."

Then, Chief Fallon came to visit again and Bob and Bonny Wentworth were with him.

Solemnly, the Chief explained another important development. "Dorothy Moorehead is the daughter of Henry and Althea Moorehead and the great-great-granddaughter of James Samuelson. As far as I know, Samuelson was Oliver Colby's lawyer." The room was silent as he went on. "If Dorothy was at Jake's house, something important must be going on."

"What would it take to get them to tip their hand?" asked Mr. Miller.

"We still have to connect them with the letters. Without that, there is no case," replied the Chief. "I can't order a search without a warrant and I really have no grounds for that."

Casey listened for a while. The voices drifted into the background as his own thoughts took hold. He moved close to Lexie and whispered close to her ear.

"Dorothy mustn't know about the coins."

Lexie paused for a moment, then said, "It sounds like Jake doesn't know where they are, either."

Casey realized that if Jake and Dorothy were to do anything with the letters, the Anne Robertson case would go into limbo again. He and Lexie would have to take matters into their own hands.

"We have to get the letters," whispered Casey.

"We have to break the code, too," said Lexie.

9

Another Adventure

It was on Friday, after school, three days after the fateful meeting with The Chief, when Lexie invited Casey into her house. They had been spending time in the Harbor Malt Shop, but it was too noisy there to concentrate on breaking the code. Work on the code was not going well. At first Casey was a bit shy. He realized that this was the first time he had been in someone's house other than Billy King's house in Shorewood. Casey was restless. It was obvious to him that Lexie enjoyed the time they were spending together, but he was frustrated that the case was not moving. He felt that he should be doing something, but what could that be?

"My mother is in her office. It used to be our dining room, but now it's filled with her art work." She poked her head into the room. "Mom, Casey's here."

Mrs. Wentworth was busy at an easel putting together preliminary charcoal sketches for another book. She got up from her perch on a stool, wiped her hands on a towel and met Casey at the door. She wore a red apron over a dark green sweater and green slacks. In her stocking feet, which was the way she was now, Mrs. Wentworth was shorter than Lexie, barely five feet three inches tall. Her complexion was dark brown, darker than Lexie. She was a very attractive thirty-eight-year-old successful artist. She held out her hand. Casey took hold with his right hand and was surprised by the firmness of her grip.

"Hello, Casey."

"Hi, Mrs. Wentworth."

"Casey and I are going downstairs."

"Your brownies are in the fridge," said Mrs. Wentworth, and with more emphasis, "the ones you made. Nice meeting you, Casey. Hope to see more of you." She smiled at Lexie and retreated to her work room.

"You made brownies?" asked Casey.

"I'm smarter than I look, you know."

"I can hardly wait."

"Want to see something?" asked Lexie.

"Sure."

Lexie led Casey into the dining room.

"Here's the award my mother got and here's the first print of the book my mother illustrated."

"Cool," said Casey. "She's really good."

"I want to do something like that some day. I'll get the brownies. The cellar is that way."

Casey went to the cellar and Lexie followed with a plastic container filled with brownies.

"Want a Coke or something?"

"Sure, that'll be fine. This is a neat playroom."

Casey removed his jacket and cap and threw them on a soft easy chair, then reached into a pocket to get the pad of paper and pencils they had been using to work on the code.

"The people who owned it before paneled it and put in lights. Somehow, I don't think Jonathan and Anne met down here."

"Who's the pool player?"

"My father. I'm not good at it. He and my mother like to play."

Casey was relieved that she wouldn't ask him to play. He found a soft easy chair in one corner of the room and watched Lexie as she opened a refrigerator and brought out two cans of Coca Cola.

"I don't need a glass," said Casey. He took a bite out of a brownie. "Mmmm. Not bad."

Lexie removed her jacket and hat, threw them on top of Casey's and went to a space under the cellar stairs to pull out a card table. As she opened it, she pointed to two folding chairs for Casey to set up. Neither had to remind the other that the reason they were there was to work on the code. Both were silent for a moment, staring at the scribbled notes they had produced.

"What's wrong?" asked Lexie. "I don't like the look on your face. My cooking can't be that bad."

"We're not getting anywhere."

"My mother once told me that when you need to solve a tough problem, sometimes you have to take a time out. Get away from it for a while."

"We don't have time for that."

"Well, what have we got so far?"

"A mess, that's what."

"Start from the beginning. Why did you rearrange the numbers?"

"I don't know. It's the first thing I thought of. I just put them in numerical order."

"Do you still think the numbers stand for letters?"

"What else could they be?"

"I don't know. I'm not very good at puzzles."

"All right, let's start from the beginning. Put the numbers back the way they were on the letter."

"There."

"OK. Twenty-one is U. Twelve is L"

Casey continued to substitute a letter for each of the numbers, using one for the letter A through number twenty-six for the letter Z.

"It spells ULAM'S NOSE," said Lexie. "Now it's beginning to make sense."

Casey and Lexie stared at the words, but saw nothing that gave them a clue.

"It's supposed to be a place, isn't it?" asked Casey.

"I don't know any Ulam, do you?"

"Maybe the letters are scrambled."

"Write down all the words you can make up and I'll do it, too."

"I got one. Son," said Lexie.

"I see lame."

"There's a noel, too."

"And Sam."

"Oh. Oh. Oh. I think I've got it," said Lexie. She stuttered as she spoke. "What does this sound like? Sam, Noel, son."

"Samuelson. That's it."

Lexie was so excited she got up screaming and threw her arms around Casey's neck as he sat at the table.

At first, Casey was embarrassed, but he, too, jumped up and they danced around the room.

"What's going on down there?" It was Lexie's mother.

"Nothing, Mom."

"Nothing? What were you screaming about?"

"Just a joke, Mom."

Casey looked at Lexie and threw up his hands.

"Now I've got you lying, too."

"I know," whispered Lexie. "Isn't it fun?"

"Only when it doesn't hurt somebody." He paused, then said, "If the code means a place, it must mean Samuelson's house, but where is that?"

"It sounds familiar. I think I can find out. Wait here."

Casey watched Lexie as she ran up the cellar stairs. He sat at the card table nervously drumming his fingers while he waited for Lexie to return.

"This is the book I told you about. It has all the owners of the historic houses in Elm Grove."

"But, how are we going to find Samuelson's."

"Now I remember. My father told me a family bought the Robertson's house."

"Look that one up."

Lexie turned to the index. The houses were listed alphabetically.

"Robertson. Here it is."

"There's Samuelson's name. He bought the house from the Robertsons. Wow."

"What do we do now?" asked Lexie.

"Let me think."

"Uh, oh. Now we're in trouble."

"Nothing is going to come of the case unless the letters turn up, right?"

"Right."

"We've got to get those letters first. There's no other way. The coins will have to wait."

"We tried Jake's house and it didn't work. He was at home."

"We just have to pick a time when we know Jake is away, that's all."

"That's all? That's all? How are we going to do that?"

"The library is open at night until nine. Jake works from three o'clock in the afternoon until at least nine thirty. He has to clean up and lock the library, so he shouldn't be home until about quarter to ten."

Casey got up and started to pace the floor. He slapped his right fist into the palm of his left hand and then he stopped and faced Lexie. "That's it. We're going in. There's no other way."

He started pacing back and forth again.

"We're doing what?" asked Lexie. "Look at me."

"We're going into Jake's house to get the letter."

"You and who else?"

"You and me. I can't do it alone and we can't tell our parents or The Chief. It's the only way."

"The only way for what? We don't have to do anything? Besides, don't you think Jake will have something to say about this?"

"That's the point. If Jake hears about the search he'll probably take off and we'll never see him again."

"And what about the coins?"

"I'll bet Jake doesn't know where the coins are. There's no telling what he'll do. Don't you see? The case is already out of sight. The Chief isn't going to do anything until January and without the letters no one will ever know that Anne Robertson is the skeleton."

"You mean the skeleton is Anne Robertson, if they find one."

"I'm sure they'll find her. We've got to get to Jake's house before the word gets out about the search. I can't do it alone."

"I must be crazy to let you talk me into these things? What's bugging you, anyway? Why can't you leave it alone?"

"I guess I owe you an explanation. Last summer a good friend of mine, Billy Keith, died. He broke into a lumber yard with his brother and two other friends, Billy fell off a roof and the others ran away and left him there. Bobby told me they heard Billy moaning and one of the others went back to help him, but Bobby thinks one of the others went back and killed Billy to keep him quiet. The police found Billy dead and the last I heard was that they were investigating it as a murder. Bobby told me what happened and he's afraid he'll be arrested, so he made me promise not to tell anyone that he was with Billy that night."

"It wasn't your fault. Why are you so worried and what does Anne Robertson have to do with it?"

"I guess I was so mad at them for leaving him like that. I'm mad at Bobby, too. He made me promise I wouldn't tell anyone. He knew I wouldn't rat on him. I shouldn't be telling you. Not telling anyone about it makes me part of it and now it's worse, you're part of it, too."

"It isn't going to bring your friend back. I still don't know what this has to do with Anne Robertson."

"I know that. Don't you see? If I don't do something about this, I'll be covering up something just like the guys who buried Anne. It's like this whole thing came up on purpose, finding all this stuff, I mean. Maybe if I can square this for Anne, I'll find a way to handle the thing about my friend. But, now you've got to promise me you won't tell a living soul about this."

"Whew. It's too heavy for me. Of course I won't tell, but does it mean we really have to break into someone's house?"

"It's the only way I know, unless you've got a better idea."

"Who, me? I'm just going along for the ride."

"Does that mean you'll go with me?"

"I guess so."

"Thanks. You've been a great friend."

"You, too."

"We can go in Monday night, after the sun goes down, around eight o'clock should give us plenty of time. The library is open until nine," said Casey.

"It's Friday. It's open until nine tonight. Why not go in tonight, have you got a hot date or something?"

"I guess we could. Why not?"

"What have I done? Wait a minute. Haven't you forgotten something?"

"What?"

"What if he's waiting on his doorstep for us?"

"We have to take that chance. He should be working."

Casey surprised himself. He had never been involved in anything dangerous. He never took charge of anything, either. At work with his father he was merely a deck hand who followed orders. When he was part of The Sandbox Gang, most of the time, he always went along with the group. Here, events were getting out of hand. He just could not let the case slip back into obscurity again. He could have ignored it all, but something inside of him kept driving him on. Maybe it was to clear his conscience about Billy, but he wondered if he was just showing off to impress Lexie. He knew for sure that he would have to find a way to clear up Billy Keith's case, too, and rid himself of his guilt and frustration.

"OK, then. So, what now?"

"I'll meet you at the bridge at eight thirty. It should be easy enough. The Chief's guard is still checking on us, but he just drives back and forth up the street, so I'll go out when he's turning around at the Coast Guard station. I'll sneak out on the ocean side."

"It's going to be really hard for me to get out of my house. If my parents decide to do something else besides watch TV, I'll be in trouble. If I'm ten minutes late, I won't be there"

"Same with me. Keep an eye out for the cruiser."

*   *   *

That night, Casey dressed for extra warmth in a dark, winter jacket, Levi's, a black, knit watch cap, warm gloves and leather boots. In the distance he heard the bells at St. Mary's Church and by the time they stopped at eight he was over the sea wall and running down the beach flashlight in hand. Lexie was at Salt Marsh Bridge waiting for him. Incredibly, Lexie wore a pair of dark-brown corduroy slacks, a tan ski jacket and tan boots. Except for her red knit cap they were dressed like twins.

"Great outfit," said Lexie.

"I saw this in a movie once, Bonnie and Clyde," said Casey.

Casey, for some reason, was lighthearted, even though he had in the back of his mind that he was heading into a dangerous situation and leading Lexie into it, too. Maybe it was just like whistling in the dark, trying to cover up the sound of his heart, which was beating like an oversized drum.

"My mother's name is Bonnie, did you know that?"

"Sorry about that. No, I didn't."

"Well, come on, Clyde, let's do it."

The weather was crisp and clear. The Causeway was neatly plowed. As they walked, the only sound they could hear was the squeak of their boots on the thin coating of packed snow. Hundreds of stars sparkled against the black night sky. Only the sliver of a crescent moon appeared over St. Mary's Church steeple. They turned right onto Oak Lane and continued until they reached the entrance to the cemetery where they paused in the light of a street lamp. The access road, unplowed, wound its way through the cemetery. It was dimly lit and barely distinguishable under the cover of snow. They were able to follow a path between the grave stones. Casey led the way into the cemetery and in less than a minute they were in total darkness. At that point, Casey, as he did before, led the way with his flashlight to Jake's back yard. When they reached the wall, he shut it off.

"Here we go again," said Lexie.

"Right. I don't think Jake is here, but I'll make sure. You stay here and I'll signal with the flashlight if it's OK to follow."

"You're leaving me alone? No way. I'm going with you."

"All right, but hold on to my jacket. It's pitch black out here. I can't use the flashlight."

Casey climbed the wall and almost lost his balance as Lexie held tight to the bottom of his jacket.

"Let go for a minute," whispered Casey. "Let me get over the wall."

"All right, but don't you leave me here."

Casey struggled to push aside bushes that lined the wall on Jake's side, then held out his hand to help Lexie.

"Where are you?" asked Casey.

"I'm here. Turn the light on for a second."

Casey did as he was told and the two joined hands.

Neither Casey nor Lexie spoke a word until they reached the dining room window where they had seen Jake and Dorothy. The house was in complete darkness.

"Jake's car is gone. No one's here," said Casey. "Let's try the back door."

Casey knew that many of the older people in town never locked their doors despite warnings. His parents spoke about it at supper when they first moved in. Some people thought the town was completely safe. They trusted their neighbors and believed that they were immune to threats of intruders. Others thought it was an unnecessary nuisance to lock their doors.

"This way," whispered Casey. "I can use the light now."

He opened a storm door, then pushed hard against the door leading into a mud room. It opened with a harsh scraping sound. Jake's house was old. That was the best thing that could be said of it. It was old outside and old inside. At one time it might have been fresh and new, but years of neglect, lack of paint and years of harsh weather left the carcass of a house that had seen better days. The back room was damp with the smell of musty old rags and the pungent odors of kerosene and garbage. An old wash machine stood by the back door. Obviously, its journey to the dump was cut short. Old boots, rusty motors, tools and bulging plastic bags, filled with trash, lined a narrow path to the kitchen door. It was unlikely that Jake could lock his kitchen door even if he wanted to. It, too, was ravaged by wear.

Casey, followed closely by Lexie, stepped into the warm kitchen. He was startled by the glow of two orange-colored spots that looked like cat eyes peering at him from the darkness. He aimed his flashlight directly at the spots and took a deep breath. The "eyes" were the openings in the door of an aged potbelly wood stove standing against the opposite wall. A fire was burning and it gave off intense heat. Obviously, this was

Jake's central heating plant. Casey moved his flashlight back and forth to survey the area. It was like stepping into the past. To his right, was a black marble sink filled with dirty dishes. Above the sink was a mirror hung between two small windows with dark- green window shades. It was common practice in Elm Grove to keep window shades pulled down in winter for extra insulation. An old ice box stood to Casey's left and next to it was a well-used refrigerator. The clatter of the refrigerator's compressor, as it suddenly started, startled Lexie as Casey turned his light away from it to explore another area of the kitchen.

"Geez, what was that?" said Lexie as she grasped Casey's arm.

"It's just the refrigerator. It's OK."

Casey took a deep breath. His heart was racing. He did his best to conceal his fear and the only way he knew how was to keep talking. "The dining room door should be over here," he said.

A closed door with a twelve-year-old calendar hanging on it was next to the opening to the dining room. The heat in the kitchen was overpowering and it made the musty odor more intense.

"Jake doesn't have a house cleaner," whispered Lexie.

"How did you guess?"

"Let's get the box and get out of here. This place gives me the creeps."

"It's in the next room," said Casey. He aimed his flashlight across the kitchen to the doorway leading to the dining room.

"You go first," said Lexie.

The dining room was more like a junk room. A dining room table in the middle of the room was surrounded by four matching antique chairs. The table top was covered with old papers, notebooks, an odd collection of hard cover and paperback books and an upright Underwood typewriter. A decrepit chandelier over the table looked like it was about to fall down. It had tarnished brass fixtures and smoked glass globes, originally designed for candles, but now it was crudely electrified. The ceiling plaster to which it was attached was cracked and stained from water leaks. The walls were covered with insipid, gray wall paper. To the left, an antique cupboard was filled with assorted glass-ware, plates, cups and saucers strewn about on the shelves. On the right was a dark mahogany credenza with its top covered with more papers and books stacked high and two of its drawers partially open with papers sticking out. Next to it was a fifth chair, part of the matching set. Above the credenza was a portrait of an elderly gentleman with an unfriendly look about him.

"Maybe that's Oliver Colby," said Casey. His flashlight created eerie shadows across the face.

"Look," said Lexie. "Here's the yearbook."

"So, Jake took it after all."

"Let's just get the letter and get out of here," said Lexie. "This place gives me the creeps."

"I know. You said that."

`Casey scanned the room with his flashlight. "The tin box was on the table, but I don't see it now."

"There it is. On that chair."

"Grab it and let's get going. I'll take the yearbook," said Casey.

Lexie opened the tin box and saw the letter. She closed the box and said, "It's here. Let's go."

Before they could get to the kitchen, a flash of light came through the dining room window. They heard the roar of a car's engine as the driver revved it up. It stopped near the back of the house, made a rattling noise and finally came to rest. Then there was silence.

"It's Jake," said Casey as he turned off his flashlight.

"What are we going to do?" asked Lexie. "I can't see a thing."

Quickly, Casey grabbed Lexie's arm and pulled her into the kitchen. He remembered the door with the calendar on it. He prayed that it was not a closet. He covered his flashlight with his hand and turned it on. The glow gave enough light so that he could see the door knob. He turned the knob but the door would not open. The door was warped and jammed tight. Casey pulled hard and the door opened with a loud scraping noise. He breathed a sigh of relief when he saw a steep stairway to the cellar. Below, it was pitch black. He turned the flashlight on.

"Down here, quick," said Casey. "I hope Jake didn't hear us."

Casey started down ahead of Lexie. They heard the car door slam as they closed the cellar door behind them. When he reached the bottom of the steps, Casey bent low to avoid hitting his head, stepped onto soft earth and motioned to Lexie to follow him. It was a shallow cellar barely high enough for them to walk bent over. It was cold and damp. A rancid odor caused Casey to choke. The light from Casey's flashlight penetrated the darkness. Ahead was a wide-open crawl space littered with objects accumulated over the years. Tin cans and rusty automobile parts were everywhere. Pieces of broken furniture were strewn about and several black plastic bags stuffed to the breaking point sat at the bottom of the stairs. Casey realized that if Jake opened the cellar door, light from the kitchen would light up the stairway and part of the crawl space. He looked to his right. There was a space against the wall away from the stairway where they could hide. Casey and Lexie crouched low and huddled together against the wall with Lexie tightly clutching the box. They were so close, when they breathed they felt the warmth of each other's breath on their faces. Casey turned his flashlight off and they waited in silence.

The muffled sound of the back door opening startled Casey and Lexie. When they heard the pounding of footsteps directly over their heads they huddled closer together and held their breath. They traced Jake's footsteps from the kitchen through the dining room and into the living room at the front of the house.

"Jake is alone," whispered Casey.

There was a moment of silence.

"What's he doing?" whispered Lexie.

Before Casey could answer, they heard a swishing sound, as if something was being dragged across the floor above them. Without warning, the cellar door opened accompanied by its loud scraping noise and a beam of light from the kitchen lit up the cellar staircase. Casey and Lexie tried to move farther away, but they were huddled against a cold fieldstone wall. Again, they clutched each other as if to try to make themselves smaller. Jake was coming down. There were footsteps on the staircase, then a scraping sound. Suddenly, the crawl space was flooded with light. Jake had pulled a string attached to a single light bulb over the stairway. He stood hunched over at the bottom of the stairs dressed in a black and red checked winter coat, a hat with earmuffs, gloves and boots laced up to his knees. Neither Casey nor Lexie could see his face as he tugged at a large object wrapped in a blanket which he took hold of and dragged to the bottom of the stairs. He rested for a moment, then, with great effort, he moved one step at a time, backwards, across the crawl space dragging the thing in the blanket behind him. He made sure that whatever it was in the blanket was fully covered. He gave it a couple of pats with a gloved hand and went back up the stairs, shutting the light off and slamming the warped cellar door behind him.

Casey and Lexie waited in the darkness. Directly over their heads they heard Jake's footsteps crossing the kitchen floor and into what they knew was the dining room. They heard the sound of a chair scraping the floor and assumed that Jake was at his table in the dining room. All of a sudden they heard a sound like thunder and Jake's muffled screams followed by the ponderous thump of a heavy object striking the floor. They heard loud stomping of footsteps back and forth from the living room to the dining room and back again, then silence. A few minutes later, which seemed like hours to Casey and Lexie, they heard the muffled scraping of the chair and then footsteps.

"He's going back into the kitchen," whispered Casey.

Casey and Lexie huddled closer together, praying that Jake would not come down again. Then, they heard the scraping noise at the back door as it opened and closed. They waited in silence, too cold and frightened to speak.

It was Lexie who broke the silence. "What was that all about?" Lexie's voice trembled with the cold and the uncertainty of what would happen next.

"Jake must have found out the box is gone."

"He must be going crazy."

"I don't know about that, but that sure looks like a body in the blanket," replied Casey.

"Where did it come from? Was it in the living room when we picked up the box?"

"It must have been there."

"What should we do?" asked Lexie. Her voice trembled again as she spoke. Her whole body was shivering. "If Jake finds us, he'll kill us, too."

"We'd better wait for a while."

"I'm freezing. I hope we don't have to spend the night down here."

"Me, too," said Casey.

Before he could say another word, they heard the sound of a car starting. It belched a few times then roared to life.

"I think Jake is leaving. He's backing out," said Lexie.

They waited in the darkness until they were certain that Jake was gone. Casey turned on his flashlight and aimed it at the place where they saw the blanket.

"That was something heavy," said Casey.

"I'm really not interested in that," said Lexie, "It's time for us to go."

"Don't you want to know what's in the blanket?"

"No way. Let's get out of here before Jake comes back."

"I think it's safe now. I have to see what's in the blanket," said Casey.

"You've got to be kidding. What's wrong with you? I want to get out of here."

"Wait at the bottom of the stairs, I'll be right there."

Casey edged his way to the blanket and uncovered one side. In the light of the flashlight, Casey saw an arm. Casey jumped back and quickly returned to Lexie.

"It's a dead body," he whispered in a state of panic.

"Was it Dorothy?" asked Lexie.

"It must be. I didn't see the face, but it must be she."

"I don't believe you did that. I'm getting out of here, now."

"Stay here for a minute," said Casey. "I'll see if the coast is clear."

Casey inched his way up the cellar stairs, put his ear to the door and, when he was satisfied that no one was in the house, he pushed the cellar door open. The kitchen light was on. He peeked into the kitchen, then waved his hand at Lexie to follow him. They wasted no time climbing the wall and leaving the cemetery behind them. When Casey and Lexie reached Salt Marsh Bridge, they paused for a moment to catch their breath.

"I don't think we should say anything about this just yet," said Casey.

"Now what? What are you thinking about? We got what you wanted. We turn the box over to The Chief and it's all over."

"No, it isn't, not until we get Dorothy's letter. And what about Dorothy? Her house will be empty."

"Dorothy's house? We're going to break into Dorothy's house? It's just across the street from where I live. What would my parents say? Besides, if Jake did away with Dorothy, he might have her letter."

"Your parents won't find out. How could they? Anyway, Dorothy was in Jake's cellar. The letter has to be at her house."

"I just don't like it. Dorothy's dead and we're breaking into her house."

"What else can we do? Do you think anyone will believe us when we tell them Dorothy's been murdered?"

"They've believed us so far, haven't they?"

"You may be right, but we'll never get a better time to go for the letter and we have to go for it before Jake has a chance to cover things up."

"He's already covered Dorothy up, with a blanket."

"Sick joke."

"I know, but I'm really nervous about all this."

"I am, too, but I can't see any other thing to do. If we tell our parents, they'll tell The Chief, The Chief will get bogged down with paper work and Jake will have time to hide or even destroy the letters."

"What if we meet Jake at Dorothy's house? Won't he be looking for the other letter? Won't he be looking for the coins, too?"

"That's why we have to do it soon."

"How soon?"

"Before tomorrow morning."

"You mean, now?"

"We can't go now. It's after nine. Our parents will be looking for us. I'm going to take the box home with me. I'll hide it in my room. We'll go in after midnight."

"I knew I wasn't going to like this."

"We have to be at home tonight so they don't suspect anything."

"Aren't you being a little dramatic about this?"

"Sure. Isn't it great?"

"I thought you were depressed and angry."

"I am."

"Right."

"Are you with me or not."

"All right. What time?"

"I'll meet you in front of your house at one."

"One o'clock in the morning? Great."

"Set your alarm or something."

"All right, see you at one."

When Casey got home, he made himself a cup of hot cocoa and went straight up to his room. The vision of the arm in the blanket was still clear in his mind. He opened the box, took out the letter and read it carefully.

"You guys were really stupid, Oliver," he muttered under his breath. He put the letter back in the box and hid the box under some clothes at the bottom of his closet. No one would think of looking there.

10

Jake

Jake Colby wanted to find the coins before any action was taken by the police. He realized that he was a fool to have shown Dorothy Oliver's letter. His best bet now would be to concentrate on breaking the code and finding the coins. He was due at work at two forty-five, but he was thinking of staying at home until he came up with a plan. At ten past two o'clock in the afternoon, Jake was sitting at his dining room table contemplating his next move when he was startled by a loud pounding on his back door. The force caused the windows to rattle. He rushed to the back door thinking some ornery children might be playing a trick on him.

Before he saw Dorothy Moorehead, Jake hollered, "What's going on out here?"

"Get out of my way, Jake," said Dorothy. She could be ill-tempered at times and this was one of those times. Before Jake could react, Dorothy pushed him aside and stormed into his living room. She stood there in the middle of the room, hands on her hips.

"I've had enough of you and your whining. I've made a decision. I don't want your money anymore. You're free," said Dorothy.

"What are you up to now?" asked Jake.

"I figured out where the coins are. I'm going to get them and get out of this town."

"You're bluffing. You don't know where they are."

"That was easy. You showed me the numbers."

Jake was stunned. How could Dorothy have memorized the numbers and broken the code so quickly?

"If you try to stop me, you'll pay the consequences."

"What are you talking about? What consequences?" Jake was furious. "The coins are mine," he shouted.

Dorothy shook her fist at him and laughed derisively. "You silly fool," she said. "If you even try to get the coins or, if anything happens to me, my letter will go to the newspaper. The whole town will know about your family and where Anne Robertson is buried."

"I don't care about that anymore. You can do what you want."

Jake was angry at himself for being taken in by Dorothy's husband who started the whole thing four years ago and after he died continuing with Dorothy. In trying to protect what was left of his family name, he agreed to pay them to keep quiet. Oliver had done enough to blacken the family name, but covering up the death of the daughter of one of Elm Grove's prominent citizens was too much for Jake to handle.

"Ah, but you wouldn't want that, would you? You wouldn't want too much more excitement around town before you get your coins. I know where they are. I'll get them and you'll have nothing."

"What do you really want? Why did you come here?"

"I want your letter, too, and I want it now. That's my insurance. Give it to me and I'll get out of your life forever."

Jake didn't take the time to tell Dorothy that he no longer had Oliver's letter. Four years of frustration turned into violent rage. Jake lashed out at her with the back of his hand. He was surprised by his own strength. Dorothy toppled over backward and hit her head on a corner of his fireplace. When she moaned and tried to get up he grabbed a pillow from his couch and covered her face and pressed as hard as he could. She made a halfhearted attempt to push Jake away, but she lost consciousness, her body falling limp. Jake gasped for breath. He paused for a moment and his anger subsided. He checked her pulse. Dorothy was dead.

"How far did you think you could go, Dorothy? Did you think I'd let you get away with the coins?"

Jake's first instinct was to hide her body, but it would take too long. He had to show up at work, otherwise he would have no excuse if he was questioned by the police, as he knew he would be. By hiding her body he could gain valuable time to carry out what he had intended to do before this happened, find the gold coins. He grabbed a blanket covering his couch and threw it over Dorothy's body. He would have to dispose of her when he got home from work.

He sat at his dining room table to rest. His head was spinning from the exertion. He put his head down between his knees to prevent passing out. Then, like a lightning bolt, a frightening thought hit him.

"Her car," he said out loud. "I forgot her car."

Frantically, he looked through her clothes for a key and found nothing. Through his dining room window, he saw Dorothy's car parked behind his. Like a man possessed, he ran outside in shirtsleeves and opened the driver's side door. The key was in the ignition. There was only one thing he could do at this hour, hide her car in his shed.

Jake's shed was the place where he stored his tools and worked on his car. It was a makeshift structure that he built himself out of scrap lumber and cinder blocks. It had a dirt floor, but otherwise it was as good as any garage, dry and large enough to drive his car in to do minor maintenance on it. He had been a garage mechanic and preferred to do his own work on his old station wagon.

After several maneuvers, he finally got Dorothy's car into the shed, but when he shut the door and turned around he was horrified by what he saw. Dorothy's car had made clear tracks in the snow. He got into his own car and drove it back and forth over Dorothy's car tracks until he was sure none could be recognized. He returned to the house, put on his jacket and hat and got back into his car.

"Got to get to work," he muttered.

Jake arrived at the library at two forty-five and went through his normal routine, a routine that Dorothy Moorehead demanded of him, of turning on the lights and heat and switching on the computer before Dorothy got there. Rebecca Stone, a retired librarian and elderly member of the Friends of the Elm Grove Library, was at the front door when Jake opened the library at three o'clock. She was there to fulfill her Friday volunteer work as she had done for several years. Also, Rebecca was qualified to act as Librarian in Dorothy's absence.

"Hello, Mrs. Stone," said Jake. "Dorothy called me. Said she was sick. Wants you to fill in for her."

"That's odd. She's supposed to call me directly."

"Don't know anythin' about that. Just that she won't be here. That's all I know."

Before Rebecca had a chance to respond, Jake immediately walked away toward the main desk without another word, ignoring Rebecca as she took off her coat. By the time she assumed her position behind the front desk, Jake was out of sight. Jake hid behind a row of shelves and peeked around the corner to see what Rebecca was doing. He breathed a sigh of relief as someone approached Rebecca to ask her a question and she led the person to another part of the library. The fewer words he spoke with Rebecca the better. She was like a sponge, picking up gossip and distributing it liberally anywhere she chose. It would not be in Jake's interest to have her probing for more information about Dorothy.

During the hours that followed until closing time, Jake tried desperately to maintain some semblance of order. Knowing that Anne Robertson was buried somewhere under the cellar floor, he avoided hiding or doing anything down there. He confined himself to the main room and the two adjoining rooms hoping that people would not notice the frantic look on his face or the perspiration soaking his shirt.

He occupied himself by mopping the floor, taking out trash and opening boxes of books while making sure he never entered an area where people might know him and be apt to start a conversation. He had nothing to fear about that. Jake had a reputation of being a grumpy sort, confining his contacts with people to simple grunts, never a smile. A few minutes before closing time, Jake hid in the Colby-Pritchard Room where he could observe the front door.

Promptly at nine o'clock, Rebecca put on her coat to leave.

"Jake," she hollered. "Jake, I'm leaving. I shut the computer off."

Jake chose not to answer. He watched Rebecca shrug her shoulders as she departed through the front door. He rushed to a front window and watched Rebecca until she got into her car and drove away. He then turned the heat and lights off, locked the front door and hurried to his car. At nine fifteen, Jake drove into his driveway and, before getting out of his car, he paused and took a deep breath.

"I've got to get rid of Dorothy's body." He muttered the same sentence over and over until the cold began to seep into his body.

"Got to hide Dorothy, put her in the cellar."

Quickly, Jake got out of his car and went directly to his living room. He wrapped Dorothy tightly in the blanket and dragged her to his cellar, unaware that Casey and Lexie were there watching him. When Jake finished with that, he double-checked everywhere in his living room to make sure there were no signs that Dorothy had been there. Completely exhausted, he sat again at his dining room table, laying his head on his arms.

"What am I going to do?"

A minute later, he raised his head and reached out toward the chair where he expected to find the box with Oliver's letter. Not finding it he moved papers and objects around, paused for a moment and looked around the room.

"It's gone," he screamed.

He cursed and screamed some more as he brushed all of the old notebooks, papers and books, including the typewriter off the table.

Sweating profusely and breathless from the exertion, he sat again. His heart was pounding so hard he thought his chest would burst

"I can't believe this happened," he muttered. "Those kids must have broken in. Now, what am I going to do? Can't think about that. Dorothy's dead. How will I find the coins? Maybe she was bluffing. Maybe she had them already. No, she said she didn't, but how did she know where they were? What am I doing? Dorothy can't be found here. Got to get her out of the cellar, but to where?"

He spent the next two hours driving around looking for a likely spot to dump Dorothy's body, but every time he reached a point of deciding, he backed down. There was always a good reason why the dumping spot would not work. Finally, exhausted, he parked his vintage Ford station wagon on the side street behind his house. This was the spot where Casey and Lexie entered the cemetery to get to his back yard.

"What am I going to do? What am I going to do?" he muttered to himself. "I didn't mean to hurt anyone, but Dorothy was just too greedy. She got money from me and then wanted the coins, too. I just couldn't let her go that far." He pounded his fist on the steering wheel. "It just wasn't right. Those two meddling kids started this whole thing. I'll take care of them as soon as I get through with Dorothy. Maybe I should just leave her in the cemetery. No, that won't do. They might connect me with her. An accident. That's what I need to make it look like an accident, but how?"

"She's dead. Got to think of something. I could throw her out of my car at the bridge and make it look like she was hit by a car. No, not at this time of night. No one would believe that. How can I get rid of her? Fire. That's it. A fire. What if she got caught in a fire at her house? I told Francis Stone that Dorothy was sick. That would do it. I know she has a gas stove. I was there once. But, how can I rig it so that I'm away from there. I need a fuse or something. A candle. That's it. I'll light a candle, turn on the gas and by the time it blows I'll be away from there."

It was almost midnight when Jake finally decided what to do about Dorothy Moorehead,

With the decision made, Jake drove home and, painfully, retrieved Dorothy's body from the cellar still wrapped in his blanket, opened the back door of the station wagon and pushed Dorothy inside. He stood for a moment looking at the huddled mass. He was exhausted and his whole body shook from the exertion. Perspiration dripped from his nose. He stumbled back into his house and returned a moment later with a flashlight. He lifted one side of the blanket and uncovered Dorothy's face, hoping that somehow she was still alive and he would not have to do what he was about to do. But that wouldn't work. He was better off now that she was dead. He covered Dorothy up again, closed the station wagon, got into the driver's seat and sat for a moment. The once clear and starry night turned colder and clouds moved in from the East. Beads of perspiration dripped from his face. Now he shivered from the cold and the dampness of his sweaty body. His heart continued to pound.

"What am I doing? How did I get myself into this mess? It's all because of the coins. It doesn't make sense. I can't think of that now. Got to get rid of Dorothy. Can't turn back now."

He took a deep breath and started the station wagon. No matter how careful he was or how many times he tried to fix it, he could not stop the engine from racing when it was first started. The accelerator always got stuck in the cold weather. The engine roared like a race car revving up for a drag race and then settled down to normal. Jake turned on the headlights and backed down his driveway. He looked both ways and proceeded slowly to Wood Road where he turned left then right onto The Causeway. As he passed over Salt Marsh Bridge, he glanced at the dashboard clock. It was twenty minutes past midnight. He slowed and came to a full stop at Sandy Point Road, then turned off his headlights.

He looked both ways, then slowly inched forward and turned onto Sandy Point Road. He decided not to stop at Dorothy Moorehead's house until he was sure the coast was clear. He drove on by and up to the circle at Sandy Point, turned around and slowly drifted down to Dorothy's house. He stopped briefly, then carefully, turned into Dorothy's driveway. Only the dim light from the street lamp lighted his way. There were high bushes on both sides of the driveway and small snow drifts left by a snow plow. He had to maneuver very slowly. He opened the window on the driver's side thinking he would see better and heard the crackling of the gravel under the car, muffled by a layer of snow left by the plow. As Jake steered the car toward the back of the house, he moved out of range of the light from the street lamp. He rolled down his window so he could spot the back corner of the house. He had to take the risk of leaving the engine running. If he had to start it the revving of the engine would surely wake up the neighborhood. He sat for a moment in the darkness. He looked toward the back porch and noticed a dim light coming through a kitchen window. Like him, the older people in the town left their doors unlocked and often they left a night light on, especially if they planned to return in darkness.

"Where's that path to the house? Darn it, why can't these guys do a better job plowing? He turned on his flashlight and pointed the light to scan the yard. He found a narrow shoveled path to the back porch then turned the flashlight off.

"There it is, but how am I going to get Dorothy into the house?" he muttered. "I just have to, that's all."

Jake took a deep breath and quietly opened his car door. He stepped into a snow drift up to his knees. The snow plow service was famous for its one-shot plowing, one run into the driveway with the plow down and then back out with the plow up. That was the routine. It left only the width of the snowplow with barely enough room to drive in and no room to get out of a car without bumping into a drift. With gravel driveways, like Dorothy's, the plow would only skim the surface to avoid pushing a load of snow and gravel to the back yard, so there was a layer of soft snow to walk in. He opened the back of the station wagon and turned on his flashlight so he could uncover Dorothy and position her so he could lift her out of the car. This done, he turned the flashlight off and stuffed it into his jacket pocket. He bent down, lifted one of Dorothy's arms and with the other around her waist, gave one tug and threw her over his right shoulder leaving the blanket behind.

"Uhhhh," grunted Jake. "I'm getting too old for this."

Jake staggered toward the back porch trying desperately to stay in the shoveled path. He reached the porch and stumbled up the stairs. The light from the kitchen was a godsend. With one free hand he opened a storm door, then the back door and stepped inside careful not to bump Dorothy's head on the way through.

"I have to get her up to her bedroom, make it look like she fell asleep reading or something."

There was no light in the living room or dining room. He shifted Dorothy's body so he could retrieve his flashlight from his pocket. In this awkward position, bent over with Dorothy over his shoulder he turned on the flashlight and threaded his way through the dining room and into the living room. In the far corner, he saw the stairs he was looking for and a light switch.

"Can't risk turnin' on any lights at this time of night."

Slowly, Jake mounted the narrow staircase pointing the flashlight on the stairs as best he could. At the top he grunted aloud, "Three doors. Which one?" He chose the closest on the left and pushed open the door. It was the corner room at the front of the house where some light from the street lamp presented Jake with enough light to see the layout of the room. There was a large double four-poster bed against the inside wall. Near the front window he spied a soft easy chair and with one extra heave he plunked Dorothy down into it. His aim was perfect. Dorothy remained in an upright position, her head thrown back against the back of the chair.

He took a deep breath again. Sweat was pouring off his face. "Got to take her coat off."

He struggled with Dorothy's limp body and finally got her coat off, found a hangar and hung it up in her closet. He paused for a moment to catch his breath.

"Now for the coins. She must have something here that will tell where they are."

Jake started in Dorothy's bedroom, opening drawers and emptying them, carefully at first, but, after several minutes, his frustration turned to anger. He rifled her closets, scattering clothes and boxes everywhere in all three upstairs rooms. He was like a man possessed, with only his flashlight to light his way, racing against the clock to find some evidence that would tell him how Dorothy knew the location of the coins, destroy the house and get away. He raced from room to room and when he had searched in vain he returned to Dorothy in a rage. He shook her dead body in frustration.

"Where are they?" he shouted at her.

He pushed her away and ran downstairs to search the living room and dining room. Frantically, he overturned everything that could move. In the kitchen he found a drawer with a pile of receipts and several envelopes. The largest of the envelopes had James Samuelson's name on it. He recognized the name, so he folded it and stuffed it into his jacket pocket. He walked back through the dining room and into the living room for one more look. Finally, he gave up and returned to the kitchen. Exhausted and dripping with perspiration he sat at the kitchen table, put his hands on his head and angrily pulled his hair.

He reached into his pocket and brought out the envelope. He expected to find a letter, but there were three documents in it. One of them was a codicil to James Samuelson's will. Since Marcus, Samuelson's son, had inherited all of the Samuelson property, James bequeathed ten gold coins to Marcus and the rest to his daughter, Penelope.

"So that's what happened. Old James kept the coins. That dirty crook. No time for this, got to get out of here," he muttered.

He stuffed the envelope into his pocket and retraced his steps to the living room. He found two thin candles, just the right size mounted in candle holders, one on each side of a mantle clock. Next to the clock was a small box of matches.

"Complete with matches. I don't believe it. Where did the time go? It's after twelve-thirty. Got to get out of here."

He took one candle, set it on a table near the dining room door and lit it.

"Goodbye, Dorothy."

He went to the kitchen and turned on four gas jets on the stove. The stove was perfect for the job, too. It was an antique, a stove with a pilot light that needed the help of matches to get it started. It was fed by refillable gas tanks mounted beside the back porch. He paused for a moment to make sure he could smell the gas, then left through the back door.

Jake hurried to his car, carefully closed the back of the station wagon and took one quick look back at Dorothy's house, then looked menacingly at Lexie's house. He rubbed his right shoulder and stretched his arms to ease the pain from carrying Dorothy.

"What's done, is done. Got to get out of here."

Carefully, Jake backed the car down the driveway and into the street, still with the headlights off. He maneuvered his way down to the intersection at The Causeway and stopped to look along The Causeway toward Casey's house.

"One more thing to do, but I can't do anything more tonight. Got to figure things out. Where are the coins?"

Reluctantly, he turned his car onto Salt Marsh Bridge and continued on home. Jake was exhausted. His shoulders ached from carrying Dorothy and as he shivered from the cold night air, he felt spasms in his back. The heater in his car was not working. He was perspiring from the physical effort during the past hour, something he was not used to. Pushing a mop and lifting a few books now and then was all the exercise Jake experienced for the past five years. He drove at a reasonable pace to get home without attracting any attention and was pleased with himself when he finally reached his driveway and parked his car. He sat for a brief moment to muster enough strength to rise and walk into his house. He eased himself, gently, out of the car and when he was satisfied that his legs would hold him and his back was done with its spasms, he moved briskly to his back door through the mud room and into his kitchen. The kitchen light was still burning the way he left it, but he noticed a big difference in room temperature. The wood fire in his pot-belly stove had almost burned out. Painfully, he brought in two logs from his back porch and stoked the fire until it got to its usual glow.

`"Got to have a hot cup of coffee," he muttered. He filled an old coffee pot with water, turned on the gas stove, measured a few spoonfuls of coffee and set the pot on the fire. Within a few minutes the pot began to percolate. "How can I find those coins?" He searched his pockets and pulled out the envelope he found at Dorothy's house. Still dressed in his winter coat and hat, Jake sat at his dining room table, cleared some of the debris away, spread the three documents in front of him. One was a copy of a receipt that James Samuelson gave to Oliver Colby when he took charge of the coins.

"That crook must have kept the coins after Oliver died. No one else knew about them."

The next document was a codicil to James Samuelson's will. Ten gold coins were passed to Marcus, his son and only heir.

"James had the coins. He only gave ten to Marcus. What did he do with the rest of them? He didn't give them back to my family."

The third document was Marcus Samuelson's will. In it he gave ten gold coins to Penelope, his daughter.

"Only ten, again. Where are the rest? Marcus didn't have them."

Jake thought of several questions. Did James tell his son how many coins there were before he wrote the codicil to his will? Marcus got the house, but he only got ten coins. What happened when Oliver died? Obviously, James covered up the fact that he possessed what should have been included in Oliver's estate. Where are the rest? I have to start with Samuelson's house."

11

Another Home Visit

Casey awoke just at the moment his alarm was set to go off. Without thinking, he reached up and shut it off. A twinge of pain reminded him that he had not fully recovered from the blow to his ribs. It was also a reminder of how he got it and the danger that awaited Lexie and him. He lay in his bed until he was sure that no one in the house was awake. He was still in his street clothes, including his boots. He switched on the small reading lamp over his bed, grabbed his ski jacket, black knit cap and flashlight, switched the light off and paused for a moment, again, to make sure no one else in the house was stirring.

Casey knew that he would have a better view of The Causeway if he left the house through the cellar. He crept slowly down the stairs. He knew his way to the kitchen very well in the dark, but he turned on his flashlight before descending the steps to the cellar. Quietly, he made his way through the maze of boxes and equipment and made sure that he avoided tripping over the stone on the floor. The Chief had not yet cleared the cellar, in fact, the police had not even started looking for clues here, but a police cruiser was still in the area under orders from The Chief to look out for any intruders. He opened the bulkhead door and carefully peered up and down the street. The faint glow of the one street light close to the entrance to the Coast Guard station cast eerie shadows on the soft blanket of new-fallen snow. The Causeway looked more like an open field of snow than a roadway. Convinced that the coast was clear, he stepped out of the bulkhead, carefully closed it and then made his way through the snow to the sea wall. He climbed onto it and looked down. It was a six-foot drop to the sandy beach, but, in the dark, it would be risky. He would not want to sprain an ankle or hurt himself here. He aimed his flashlight and turned it on, then jumped with the ray of light to guide him. As soon as he hit the beach, he turned the flashlight off and ran down the beach toward Lexie's house.

Usually, it took Casey at least thirty minutes to shake out the cobwebs after awakening from a sound sleep, but at this hour of the morning, the crisp, cold air, cleared his head. Gentle, rolling waves drifted onto the beach and receded. He reckoned the tide would be high in about one hour. He took deep breaths to inhale the clear, cold salty air. Large clumps of seaweed floated in with the tide and gave off an unmistakable odor. By the time he reached a safe distance from his house he was fully revived. He moved off the beach onto The Causeway, quickened his step and arrived at the front of Lexie's house on time. The walkway to the front porch was clear of snow. Piles of shoveled snow lined both sides of the walkway.

Casey approached the front porch and whispered "Lexie, are you there?"

Lexie was hiding on the porch behind a row of shrubs which cast dark shadows from the street lamp in front of Dorothy's house. She met Casey at the bottom of the stairs.

"I'm here, but I don't know why."

"We'd better go around to the back of Dorothy's house. Her front porch light is still on."

"Do you think it was Dorothy that Jake took out of his house?"

"I'm pretty sure."

"Then he might have dropped her off here."

"Not a chance. He wouldn't be that stupid."

"I just don't want to stumble on a dead body. This is giving me the creeps."

"Just stay close behind me. If I stumble on a body, you can help me up."

"Thanks a lot."

Casey led the way through a tall hedge and into Dorothy Moorehead's yard. He turned on his flashlight and saw that there was a clear path of undisturbed snow to the back of the house. The light from the street lamp lit part of the way along the side of the house. A window in the living room flickered with a soft, glowing light. Casey carefully approached the window and looked in.

"There's a lighted candle in the living room," he whispered.

"Then someone's at home. Let's get out of here."

"I can't see any other lights on in the house, just the candle."

"Maybe Dorothy went to bed and left it burning."

"I don't think anyone is at home. I'm sure Dorothy was in that blanket and I bet Jake brought her here. Let's try the back door."

"Wait a minute," said Lexie.

"What's wrong?"

"Even if no one's at home where are we going to look? This is a big house. What if Dorothy has her letter locked in a safe or something?"

"I just know we have to get in there before Jake does."

"How do you know he hasn't been here already?"

"I don't know. I'm sure he isn't here now. I didn't see any cars on the street, did you?"

"I guess not. Let's get this over with. Where do we go from here?"

"Through the back door. People don't lock their doors around here, so we'll try that first."

Casey aimed his flashlight toward the back porch.

"There's a light on in the kitchen. Someone must be home," said Lexie.

Casey climbed over a pile of shoveled snow and quietly stepped up onto the porch and gazed through the window while Lexie waited for him.

"It's all right," Casey whispered. "There's no sign of life."

"You mean you hope there's no sign of death."

"Funny. Let's go."

Casey took Lexie's hand to guide her over the pile of shoveled snow and up the porch stairs to the back door. There were two doors. One was a glass-paneled storm door, the other the main door into the kitchen. The inner door had a pane of glass about three feet square covered with a curtain. Casey could see through the curtain into the kitchen. There was a dim light on over the stove and what looked like a candle burning in the room at the front of the house. He turned off his flashlight and very carefully pulled on the handle of the storm door. It creaked and groaned as Casey pulled it open. He turned the knob on the inner door and was relieved when the door gave way.

"It's open. So far, so good," said Casey.

"That's easy for you to say. I want to get out of here."

Casey stepped into the warmth of the kitchen.

"It smells like garlic in here," said Casey.

"It doesn't smell like garlic to me, it's gas."

Casey looked toward the stove. He heard a faint hissing sound and realized that the gas was on in the stove, but no fire on the burners.

"Holy smoke," cried Casey, "The place is filled with gas. Jake must have been here ahead of us. Shut the gas off and open some windows. I'll get the candle."

Casey rushed into the next room, the dining room and into the living room. He blew out the candle and turned on a floor lamp.

"I can't open the windows," said Lexie, "They're stuck. Help me."

Both acted quickly. It took a great effort because each window had a storm window to push open. With all the downstairs windows open, the temperature in the house dropped to where Casey and Lexie could see each other's breath in the freezing cold.

"I think we have a problem," said Lexie. "Look at this. It looks like an earthquake hit the place."

Casey and Lexie looked at the devastation in the living room. Tables and chairs were turned over, picture frames smashed, lamp shades crushed, pillows and cushions torn and strewn about. Pieces of broken chinaware littered the floor in the living room and dining room.

"This is unbelievable," said Casey. "It had to be Jake. Maybe Dorothy's here. Jake must have set this up so that the house would blow up to cover up Dorothy's body."

"He wanted to use the candle as a timer so he could be away when the place blew up. When the house filled with gas, pow."

"We could have been blown up, too."

"You're right about that."

"And to think I live right across the street. What do we do now? There's no one here."

"Dorothy could be upstairs."

"There's the stairs to the second floor." Lexie pointed to one corner of the living room.

"You wait here. I'll go upstairs and look."

"And leave me down here alone. Not on your life."

Casey found a light switch which turned on the lights at the bottom and top of the stairs.

"I don't think anyone will care if the lights are on," said Casey.

Lexie nodded and followed Casey up the stairs. At the top of the stairs, there were three doors. One directly across from the top of the stairs, which was ajar and one to the left and one to the right, both shut. Casey pushed open the center door. It was the bathroom. Lexie opened the door to the left and peeked in.

"Uh, oh," said Lexie.

"What's the matter with you?" asked Casey

"There's someone in there."

Casey opened the door just enough to put his head into the room. The silhouette of what looked like a person in a chair was back lit by the light from the street lamp. He opened the door and a stream of light from the hallway shone directly into the face of Dorothy Moorehead. He saw a table lamp and turned it on.

"It's Dorothy," cried Lexie.

"See if she's alive."

"Why me?"

"You're a woman."

"What?"

"You're a woman, you check her out."

"I don't believe this."

Cautiously, Lexie touched Dorothy's hand. "It's ice cold." Gently at first, she put her hand on Dorothy's shoulder and shook Dorothy, then pushed harder. Dorothy's head slumped and she began to slide downward. Lexie had to push her back into the chair to keep her from falling to the floor.

"Is she dead?" asked Casey.

"She's dead. Thanks a lot."

As Lexie walked away, Dorothy slumped sideways and slid onto the floor.

"Oh no. We've got to put her back the way she was," said Casey.

"No way. You do it or leave her that way. I'm not touching her again. This place is giving me the creeps. Let's get out of here."

"OK. Leave her alone. Look at this place. Jake really trashed it," said Casey. "I'll call 911. I saw the phone in the kitchen. Do you want to stay here?"

"'Are you kidding?"

Casey went to the kitchen and Lexie stayed in the living room and sat down near the fireplace. In a few moments Casey joined her.

"I'm freezing. I'm going to close the windows."

"I'll help. I called 911. Jake must have been looking for Dorothy's letter and the coins," said Casey.

"I wonder if he found them."

The two sat in silence for a few short moments, staring at the empty fireplace. Nearby was a log holder filled with firewood, four heavy logs and kindling. A piece of brown leather dangled from the middle of the pile.

"An ambulance should be here in about ten minutes," said Casey. As he spoke, on an impulse, he leaned forward and pulled on the piece of leather, but whatever was attached to it was stuck under the logs. He lifted the top log and pulled again. Out popped a small leather pocketbook.

"What's that?" asked Lexie.

Casey held the pocketbook in his hand and shook it.

"Something heavy in here. Hold out your hands."

He opened the purse and emptied the contents into Lexie's hands. Ten gold coins poured out.

"It's the coins. We've found the coins. How do you like that?" said Lexie. "These are really old. Look at the year, 1857 and there's ten of them. These must be really valuable."

"But the letter said there was a lot more. Where are the rest of them?"

"Maybe Dorothy spent them."

Casey squeezed the purse. There was something else inside, a small brown envelope and, inside that, a tightly folded letter. He read a few lines to himself and stood with a dazed look on his face.

"What's wrong? What is it?" asked Lexie.

"It's Jason Pritchard's letter. You read it."

Lexie took the letter. Like the other, it was written in long hand, not quite as fancy as the other.

I, Jason Pritchard, being of sound mind, now confess my part in a scheme executed with the devil.

On April 10, 1898, while returning from business in the capitol, my horse struck and killed Anne Robertson, the girl my son said he would marry one day. It was an accident on a stormy night, but I feared that dire consequences would follow and ruin my partnership with Oliver Colby.

In a state of disarray, I went to Oliver's house and there we conspired to cover up the deed. We buried Anne in the library now under construction. I have taken a solemn oath with Oliver not to reveal our evil doings, but I am fearful that I will be left alone to suffer the consequences of the affair should it come to light.

In all honesty, I was not in full agreement about this, but the deed is done and there is no turning back. Who knows why the devil chose me to suffer as I have.

I affix my signature to this true confession this Eleventh day of April in the year 1898.

Jason Pritchard

"Is he kidding?" asked Lexie. "He says he suffered. What about Anne? And to think they got away with it. What a pair of creeps."

"That's really bad, isn't it?"

"Anything else in there?"

"Just a scrap of paper. Oh, oh. Look at this. It's the code. Dorothy broke the code."

"Samuelson."

Before they could go on, the flashing red lights of an ambulance danced on the living room ceiling followed by flashing blue lights from a police cruiser. Casey put the coins and the letter back into the purse, shoved it into his jacket pocket. He put the scrap of paper in another pocket and ran to the front door to meet the Emergency Medical Team before they got to the front door.

"She's upstairs. It's Dorothy Moorehead, from the library. She's dead. My friend, Lexie and I found her. She's in the bedroom on the left, at the top of the stairs."

A man and a woman on the EMT team and a policeman rushed upstairs.

"What are we going to do now?" asked Lexie.

"What do you mean?"

"How are we going to explain how we found her at one-thirty in the morning?"

"Let's get out of here. We'd better get your parents up."

"They're going to love this."

Lexie led the way across the street and into her living room.

"Wait here. I'll get them up."

Lexie went upstairs and returned a few minutes later, followed by her parents, both in bathrobes.

"What's going on?" asked Mrs. Wentworth.

"There's an ambulance at Dorothy Moorehead's house," said Mr. Wentworth, looking out the front window. He saw the red flashing lights from the ambulance and blue lights from the police cruiser. "You stay here. I'm going out to talk to the policeman," said Mr. Wentworth.

"What's going on, Lexie," said Mrs. Wentworth.

"It's Dorothy Moorehead," said Lexie.

Lexie explained how Casey and she entered Dorothy's house and what they found. As she finished what she had to say, the ambulance drove away, but the police cruiser, with its blue lights still flashing, stayed. Mr. Wentworth returned to the group.

"Come with me, Casey," said Mr. Wentworth. "The policeman wants you to talk to The Chief."

Mr. Wentworth lead Casey to the police cruiser and the policeman showed him how to use the police radio.

"Hello, Chief Fallon."

"What have you been up to now?" The Chief's voice was firm, but he did not seem to be upset.

"Lexie and I found Dorothy Moorehead. She's dead."

"I know that. Look, I don't have time to get into the details. Be in my office at eleven today."

"Yes, sir. We'll be there."

"Put Joe back on."

Casey handed the microphone to the policeman and, after a brief conversation, he signed off.

"The Chief, a photographer and the coroner will probably be here soon," said Officer Thompson. "They didn't move Dorothy. More police will be coming to seal the house off as a crime scene. I told him you would be at the station today to answer questions. Now, tell me what happened."

"We went in to find the second letter and found Dorothy dead," said Lexie. "The gas was on and a candle burning. If we hadn't gone in, the house would have blown up and Dorothy with it."

"And your parents don't know anything yet?" asked Mr. Wentworth.

"I was just going home to tell them."

"Show them what we found, Casey," said Lexie.

Casey handed over the purse. "Look inside. There's coins and a letter."

Mr. Wentworth examined the coins and handed them to his wife, then read the letter out loud.

"These coins must be valuable. Look at the date on each one, 1857," said Mrs. Wentworth.

"This letter proves that Anne is the skeleton," said Casey.

"Get in our car. We're all going to your house. I want your father and mother to see this," said Mr. Wentworth.

"I'll go change," said Mrs. Wentworth.

"I will, too. As long as we're up, we might as well wake up the rest of the town."

*   *   *

The short ride to Casey's house seemed like an eternity to Casey. The flashing red lights of the ambulance and the blue cruiser lights in front of Dorothy Moorehead's house were stunning reminders of the night he saw the lights at Billy Keith's house. He was back in the middle of a murder and having to face his father and mother about his being out on the street at this hour of the night. Things were not working out according to the way Casey thought they would. Instead of a simple case of uncovering an age-old mystery he found himself with a threat to his life and now a murder. Lexie sat with him in the back seat. As they approached the intersection of The Causeway near the bridge, light from the street lamps briefly lit up Lexie's face. He glanced at Lexie's expressionless face. She turned toward him and she smiled at him as she had done before.

When they arrived at his house, Casey said, "I have to go through the cellar to get into the house. I'll be right back. If you wait here, I'll get my parents up and let you in through the front door."

Using his flashlight, Casey entered the cellar through the bulkhead and ran up the stairs into the kitchen then upstairs to wake his parents.

"What's going on now?" said Mr. Miller.

"Mr. and Mrs. Wentworth and Lexie are here. We've got another problem," replied Casey. "I'll tell them you'll be right down."

"I'd better get Kathy up, too. She'd never forgive us if we left her out of whatever is going on," said Mrs. Miller.

Casey hurried to get downstairs, more for getting out of his parents' room as quickly as possible than for any other reason. He would rather face his parents with someone else around. Halfway down the stairs he remembered the box and went back to his room to get it, then bounded down the stairs to open the front door for the Wentworths. Mr. and Mrs. Miller and Kathy followed soon after in their bathrobes.

"Hello, Bob," said Mr. Miller.

"Hello, Ed. Looks like a bad one this time."

Kathy rubbed her eyes and said, "Is this another one of your exciting dates?" She looked at Lexie.

"It's worse this time," said Lexie.

"I'll put a pot of coffee on," said Mrs. Miller. "I have a feeling we're going to be up for a while. Start without me, I'll listen from the kitchen."

"You'd better start from the beginning," said Mr. Miller.

Casey explained as briefly as possible why they went into Dorothy Moorehead's house and what they found.

"They picked up Dorothy just a few minutes ago," said Mrs. Wentworth. "She's dead, murdered."

"And we know it was Jake Colby who did it," said Lexie.

"He was trying to get rid of Dorothy Moorehead. An explosion and fire would cover his tracks," said Casey.

"Slow down. What do you mean, get rid of Dorothy Moorehead?" asked Mr. Miller.

"We didn't tell you that we saw Jake put Dorothy's body in his cellar," replied Casey.

"I said it before," said Kathy, "You sure know how to treat a girl on a date."

"We got into Jake's house last night," said Casey.

"And he came back and we got trapped," said Lexie.

"So, we hid in his cellar. Jake came down and there was something heavy wrapped up in a blanket. He put it down there."

"We know it was Dorothy Moorehead in the blanket, Casey looked."

"You saw Dorothy dead?" asked Mr. Wentworth.

"Not all of her, just her arm, but we know it was her," said Casey.

"We got the box with the letter in it at Jake's house. See, here it is." Casey handed the letter to his father.

"There's something in here about gold coins," said Mr. Miller.

"He's got something else to show you," said Mr. Wentworth.

"We found this leather pouch," said Casey.

Mr. Miller looked in the pouch. "Are these the coins?"

"Only a few of them," said Lexie.

Casey poked Lexie's arm before she could tell about the code.

"What do these numbers mean?" asked Mrs. Miller.

"We didn't tell you about that," said Lexie

"I don't believe this," said Mrs. Miller. "Why didn't you tell us about the coins, Casey?"

"I didn't think it mattered until now," said Casey. He knew it was a half truth. When he first told his parents about the letter, he had no idea it would lead to murder.

"What do you mean, until now?" said Mrs. Wentworth.

"Have you told us everything?" asked Mr. Miller.

Casey desperately wanted to change the subject. He still thought he could recover the rest of the coins and get a reward.

"Dorothy's house is really trashed. Jake tore the house apart. We think he was trying to get Dorothy's letter."

"Are you sure it's Jake doing all this?" asked Mrs. Wentworth.

"Well, Jake had the box, right?" asked Casey. "We know he had Mr. Colby's letter. Dorothy Moorehead had Jason Pritchard's letter and Jake and Dorothy were arguing at Jake's house."

"We can't do anything at this time of night, I mean morning. The Chief has the case now. Let's get back to bed. I still have to go to work tomorrow, I mean today," said Mr. Wentworth.

"Right we'll have to talk with The Chief," said Mrs. Wentworth.

"He's busy at Dorothy Moorehead's house. He'll be busy there for a while. Casey talked with him. The Chief told Casey to meet him at his office at eleven. He wants Lexie there, too. I think it can wait 'til then."

"All right," said Mr. Miller. "My wife and I will go with them."

"I'll go, too," said Mrs. Wentworth.

While the Millers and Wentworths talked and moved toward the front door, Casey drew Lexie aside.

"There's one thing we have to do now," said Casey.

"Uh, oh. Here we go again. Every time you say something like that I'm going on a trip into someone's house," said Lexie.

"Wouldn't you like to find the rest of the gold coins?" asked Casey. "Meet me at the bridge in an hour."

12

Fire and Brimstone

Casey went to his room and sat on his bed in the dark, waiting for his parents and Kathy to go to sleep. He heard his parents talking in their bedroom for a few minutes, then there was silence. He traced Kathy's footsteps to her room, to the bathroom and back again and her door closing. Then, he heard her door open again followed by a light tapping on his door. He opened his door just enough to see Kathy and to hide the fact that he was fully dressed.

"Casey, are you all right?" she whispered. "Can I come in for a minute?"

"Not now, Kath, I'm really bushed."

"I know I've been kidding you a lot lately and I just want to say I'm sorry."

"It's all right, Kath, you don't have to say anything." Casey was anxious for Kathy to go to bed.

"Are you sure you're all right?"

"I'm fine, Kath, good night."

"Well, OK. I just wanted to say I'm sorry."

"Good night, Kath."

Casey closed his door and listened for signs that Kathy had gone to her room. When he heard Kathy's door, close, he opened his again and waited until the light under Kathy's door went out. Gently, he closed his door again and shut his bedroom light off. He would have to wait for at least ten minutes until he could be sure everyone was asleep.

In darkness, he gazed out his window at the ocean. To the North, he could see the intermittent light from the Harbor Point Lighthouse about a mile away. It flashed twice, then paused, then flashed three times, then paused, then flashed twice again. At times like these, alone in his room, Casey would become mesmerized by the sky and ocean merged into a deep blackness interrupted by the steady, monotonous blinking of the light from the lighthouse. There was no sign of life out there. He wondered what it would be like to live his entire life in this kind of cocoon, protected by the four walls of his room and only his window to view the outside world. His hypnotic state was broken by the pinging sound of the alarm clock he set in case he fell asleep. Quickly, he silenced it. He paused for a moment to reflect on what he was about to do. He had a plan and it was just as daring as before. It had to be carried out now. The stakes were very high. His only fear was about getting Lexie more deeply involved. He would give her a chance to back out, but deep down he hoped she wouldn't. Casey felt more sure of himself with someone with him. If she did back down, he would probably back down, too.

Casey put on his ski jacket and put his flashlight in his pocket. Gingerly, he opened his door, just a crack at first, then, satisfied that no one was awake, he crept silently down the stairs to the kitchen. He took his usual route through the cellar and out through the bulkhead. Again, he paused at the doorstep to make sure the police cruiser was out of sight, then made his way to the sea wall. There was only a slight breeze blowing in from the ocean. Although the temperature was in the mid twenties, it seemed warmer by comparison to the last few days. The glow of a half moon shone through the overcast sky. He jumped off the wall, ran along the beach and crossed the short stretch of reedy grass to

The Causeway. Before he turned toward the bridge, Lexie stepped out from behind a tree.

"I had to meet you here. The bridge is too out in the open. I barely made it out of the house. I thought my parents would never quiet down. They talked forever about this. What do we do now, as if I didn't know? Whose house do we break into this time?" She threw the questions at Casey in rapid-fire succession like she had taken a pep pill.

"Slow down," said Casey. "You're really wired."

"I know. I'm really nervous this time. I still haven't gotten over touching Dorothy. That really gave me the creeps. And you touching the arm in the blanket blew me away. Where are we going?"

"Samuelson's," answered Casey. "But, I had time to think about this. You really don't have to go into this if you don't want to. I won't care if you back out."

"Back out? You make it sound like I'd be chicken if I did."

"No, I didn't mean it that way. I'm just afraid I got you into this and I don't want anything to happen to you."

"Thanks, but no thanks. I'm no chicken. You couldn't keep me out if you gave me all the gold coins. Samuelson's? Why there? No, let me guess. You think the coins are in there?"

"It's the only place that makes sense. I think lawyer Samuelson held onto them when Oliver Colby died."

"I just hope there aren't any dead bodies laying around. If there are, you'll never get me to touch one again. Well, let's not stand around, let's get to it."

Casey had to quicken his step to keep up with Lexie. He followed her up Sandy Point Road. There were only three street lamps on Sandy Point Road, one at the intersection near the bridge, one in front of Lexie's house, which also was in front of Dorothy Moorehead's house. The third one was at the circle at Sandy Point. When they reached Dorothy Moorehead's house they noticed yellow tape draped across the front porch and across the entrance to the driveway.

"They've got Dorothy's place sealed off as a crime scene," said Casey. "Just like on TV. And to think we were the ones who found her."

Lexie, again, took the lead and Casey followed.

"Samuelson's is up here to the left," said Lexie. She used a quieter tone of voice.

Neither of them spoke until they arrived at the front yard of the Samuelson house. Both of them stopped at the same time to survey the landscape. The house was hidden behind tall bushes now covered with a layer of four inches of snow. The entrance to the walkway to the front porch was narrowed by the overhang of thick bushes which had not been trimmed for several seasons. There were no lights on in the house and no light from any of the street lamps. The house stood between the street lamp in front of Dorothy Moorehead's house and one that stood at the end of Sandy Point Road, at least fifty yards away.

About thirty feet from the front entrance was a narrow, unplowed driveway well hidden behind more large bushes. Drifts of windblown snow were much deeper on the driveway side of the house. Unlike Dorothy Moorehead's house, the back yard at Samuelson's house was open to the sea and ended at a cliff.

"This place looks like my house," whispered Lexie.

"What are you whispering for?" asked Casey.

"I don't know. I just thought it was what I was supposed to do at this time of night." She spoke her normal tone of voice. "Are we supposed to break into this place?"

"We may have to. It looks like it's boarded up."

As Casey guessed, the house was boarded up for the Winter. All of the windows and doors were covered with plywood panels specially cut to fit. Casey turned on his flashlight and led the way through the bushes at the front entrance.

"We'll never get in through a window or door. Look at this place. It's sealed up tighter than a drum."

"Somehow I know you'll find a way in."

"My friends in the Sandbox Gang knew how to break into a school. They went in through the cellar."

"This old house has a fieldstone foundation like my house. If the cellar windows are like ours you should be able to force one of them open. Our playroom windows were done over, but I know the rest haven't been touched for a while."

Large clumps of snow fell on them as Casey and Lexie pushed their way through a tall, thick hedge lining the front walkway. He found a cellar window midway between the front and the back of the house. He knelt down and tested the window by pushing hard with his hand. It did not budge.

"This will take a little work." Casey sat in the snow and placed his feet against the window frame and pushed. The window was hinged at the top. The lock at the bottom was rusty, so, when he stomped harder with his foot against the bottom, it swung open. He and Lexie paused for a moment to make sure no one heard the noise.

"I don't think anyone could hear that. We're pretty far from any houses," said Lexie.

"This will be a tight fit, but I think I can make it," whispered Casey.

"Now you're whispering."

Casey aimed his flashlight at Lexie's face and, without a reply, knelt down and put his head through the window. He flashed his light around the cellar and below the window. It was a six-foot drop to the cellar floor. He made sure that there was nothing under the window for him to stumble on.

"Here I go,"

Casey sat again and inched forward until his feet were inside the window. He then turned over on his stomach and slid backward through the window until his waist was even with the window sill. Gradually, he let himself down while he held tight to the sill. He paused for a moment, then let go and dropped to the cellar floor.

"I'm in," he said. "That was easy. Come on down."

Lexie followed Casey's lead and Casey guided her down. When both of them were inside, he flashed his light in various directions to see what was in the cellar. It was filled mostly with summer lawn furniture, umbrellas and beach chairs neatly stacked. The space was surprisingly clean and uncluttered.

"What now?" asked Lexie. "Where do you think we should look first?"

"Good question. I don't know."

"You don't suppose they'd be hidden in the foundation, like at your place."

"Not a bad idea. I think they've been hidden for a hundred years. That lawyer, Samuelson, may have died and not told anyone where he hid them. If they were found, why would Jake be after them?"

"Then we should start here."

Lexie saw a string attached to a light fixture and pulled on it. "Nothing. Everything is off for the winter."

"You hold the light and I'll check out the stones in the foundation to see if any are loose. Let's start with this corner and work our way around."

Except for a few pieces of furniture, Casey was able to make his way along the cellar wall unimpeded. He felt every stone in the foundation hoping that one would come loose. Lexie followed him with the light. After checking two sides, Casey came to the farthest corner from the street. He felt one stone move at the top of the foundation.

"I found a loose stone," said Casey.

"My heart is pounding so hard I think it's going to explode."

"Shine the light a little closer. I'm going to need something to stand on."

"Here's a table. Try this." Lexie dragged a small iron table to the wall.

Casey stood on the table and grasped the stone in both hands. "It's a big one and it's stuck. See if you can find any tools in this place. I think I'll need a crow bar. Someone has patched it up with cement."

Lexie flashed the light around the cellar and spied a small wooden chest that looked like a tool box. Beside the box there were other tools on a makeshift bench. One was a mason's trowel.

"Maybe this will work," said Lexie as she handed Casey the tool.

"Stand back. I'm going to chip the cement away from the stone."

Casey hammered away at the cement surrounding the stone until he was able to grasp the stone with both hands.

"Watch out. I'm going to let it drop. It's too heavy."

Casey got down off the table, pushed it away and reached up to grab the stone. He worked it back and forth again and the stone came crashing to the floor.

"Do you want to take the first look?" asked Casey.

"No. You go ahead. You've earned it."

Casey stood on the table again. The hole left by the stone was at eye level. He took the flashlight and peered into the hole.

"There's a big clump of something in there about an arms length in."

"Can you reach it?"

"My jacket makes my arm too big."

Casey took off his jacket and reached into the hole as far as his arm could stretch. The stones surrounding the hole were ice cold and damp. He felt particles of cement and then his fingertips caught hold of something smooth, like leather.

"There's some kind of leather bag in here. Wait, I think there are two of them. There, I've got one. It's really heavy. Boy, what a stink."

"Oh, my gosh, oh, my gosh, oh, my gosh," stuttered Lexie.

Casey pulled the leather bag out of the hole and set it on the table. It looked like an oversized tobacco pouch, about the size of a plastic grocery bag pulled closed at the top with a leather thong which was tied into a knot. The leather was covered with green mold.

"Whew, this thing smells bad. It's been here for a while," said Lexie.

Casey lifted it again, but took care to put his hand under it. He shook it gently. Lexie squeezed the bottom. They were both convinced the pouch held some coins.

"Open it, quick," said Lexie. "I'm dying to see this."

"It's really cold in here. Let me get my jacket on. I need a knife or a screwdriver or something."

Lexie went back to the old chest and found an old carving knife. "I don't know how sharp this is."

Casey inserted the point of the knife into the knot, worked it back and forth and undid the knot. He pulled open the pouch and reached inside. He brought out a fistful of coins.

"Hold the light," said Casey.

"Have you ever seen anything so beautiful?" asked Lexie. "They have 1857 on them, too."

The coins glittered in the light.

"This bag must weigh at least twenty pounds."

"What should we do?"

"I'll get the other bag out and then we'll have to take them to your house."

"You're not taking them anywhere," they heard a voice shout from the cellar stairs.

Casey and Lexie froze in the bright glare of a flashlight. They shielded their eyes from its brightness. Casey aimed his flashlight toward the voice. Out of the darkness of the cellar came Jake.

"How did you get in here?" asked Casey.

"Through the back door. It was easy. They didn't board that up."

"But, how did you know we were here?" asked Lexie. Her voice trembled as she spoke.

"I didn't until you banged on the window. I heard you from upstairs and while you were crawling through the window I hid on the stairs. I was curious to know what you were up to. You led me to my coins."

Casey noticed that Jake had no weapon. He kept talking with Jake to kill time until he could think of something to do. Without a weapon Jake could not do too much, but he was much bigger and stronger than Casey. Lexie and he could make a run for it, but the way they came in was out of reach. They would have to go up the cellar stairs, leave Jake behind and go for the police. Casey gently took Lexie by the arm and backed away from the stairway. As he hoped, Jake came down off the stairs.

"What are you going to do now?" asked Lexie. "Are you going to kill us, like you killed Dorothy?"

"Dorothy got too greedy. It was an accident. I didn't mean for her to die."

"What do you mean, she got greedy? What did she have to do with you?" asked Casey, hoping Jake would keep talking.

"You stole the box from Casey's cellar, didn't you?" asked Lexie.

"I knew it was there all along, but I waited too long. I should have gone in when the house was empty."

"You were the one who left the note threatening to kill me," said Casey.

Jake became irritable. "I only meant to scare you, "he said gruffly. "If you two hadn't stuck your nose in we wouldn't be here now."

Casey leaned toward Lexie and whispered in her ear and at the same time flashed his light toward the cellar stairs.

"Let's make a run for it. He can't do anything."

Casey grabbed Lexie by the arm and steered her to the stairway, but Jake was too quick. He, too, grabbed Lexie's arm and he pulled her toward him so abruptly that Casey let go.

"Thought you could run away," said Jake. "Now, quiet down or your friend will get the same as Dorothy."

Jake held Lexie with her back toward him and his left forearm around her neck. With his other hand he aimed his flashlight straight into Casey's face, then he aimed it away into a corner of the cellar.

"Over there," said Jake. "There are umbrellas tied up. Get the ropes off them, now, or I'll start hurting her," shouted Jake.

Casey saw the look of fear and pain in Lexie's face. He would have to obey Jake until he could think of something to do. He wandered through the cellar, pushing aside the lawn furniture, shining his light to and fro desperately looking for a piece of rope. Was Jake going to make him tie Lexie up? Casey began to hatch a plan. He found what he was looking for, the ropes used to keep the beach umbrellas folded. He undid the knots and went back to Jake and Lexie. He threw the ropes at Jake.

"Don't get wise with me," yelled Jake. "Pick up the ropes and tie your friends hands behind her back."

As he spoke, he turned Lexie around while keeping his arm around her throat.

"Put your hands together."

Lexie did as she was told and Casey tied her hands. He never expected that Jake would be so naive about this. Casey learned knot tying very well under his father's teaching on their fishing trips. He tied Lexie's hands with a sheet bend. With one pull at a loose end Lexie would be free.

"Step back," said Jake to Casey.

Jake turned Lexie around again and forced her to bend her knees.

"Lie down," said Jake to Lexie. "On your stomach."

Jake held his grip on Lexie as long as he could. When Lexie was on her stomach Jake shifted and put his foot on Lexie's neck.

"Now, tie her feet or I'll crush her head." Jake was getting more agitated. "Do it. Now."

Casey held Lexie's feet together and tied them with the same knot. Jake was too irritated to pay attention to what Casey was doing.

"Come here," said Jake. "Turn around."

With one foot on Lexie's neck, Jake took another piece of rope and tied Casey's hands behind his back.

"You, too. Get on your stomach."

Casey did as he was told and Jake tied his feet.

"Now, let's see you get out of this one."

Jake took Casey's flashlight, shut it off and threw it to a far corner of the cellar. He aimed his light toward the table on which Casey had put the leather pouches. He grabbed one, tucked it under his arm, then grabbed the second and took three steps up the stairs. He paused and flashed his light back onto the two prostrate forms.

"Goodbye," said Jake. "Finally, I'm through with you."

Jake disappeared up the stairs leaving Casey and Lexie in total darkness. They heard the cellar door slam shut and Jake's footsteps on the floor above, then silence.

"He's going to do the gas thing? Isn't the gas shut off?"

"He knows about the gas tanks. All these places have them. He can turn it on outside, just like a barbecue tank."

"Here we are again. In another cellar," said Lexie.

Casey inched his way toward her voice until their bodies met in the darkness.

"Can you turn on your side?" asked Casey. "We need to get back to back. I can get your hands free."

Lexie turned and Casey backed up against her. Their hands met and Casey found an end of the rope and pulled. The knot came loose.

"How did you do that?" asked Lexie.

"Just a trick I learned. Untie my hands."

When both were untied, Casey did not hesitate.

"We have to go out through the window. We don't have time to go upstairs."

"I think the window is over here. I can feel cold air," said Lexie. "Take my hand."

Casey grabbed Lexie's hand and he felt her pull at him. He, too, felt a draft of cold air.

"Reach up there," said Lexie.

Casey felt his way up the fieldstone wall until he found the window.
"You first," said Casey. "Step into my hands."
"I'm not going to argue this time. Where are you?"
"Here. I've got my hands together."

After a few seconds of reaching out and feeling her way in the dark, Lexie put one foot on Casey's hands. He lifted her up and she found the window. She had to swing it open from the bottom. She grabbed the outer edge of the sill and pulled herself up. As she did, the window fell onto her back.

"I'm stuck," she said. "The window fell down on me. Let me down a bit."

Casey dropped his hands down and when he did, Lexie was able to push the window up with her left elbow while pulling herself up with her right hand. She struggled that way, helped by Casey pushing at the same time, until she freed herself and rolled over in the snow. She poked her head back through the window and whispered to Casey.

"I'm out. Give me your hand."

Casey groped in the darkness and felt Lexie's hand. She guided his hands to the window sill until he could grab hold and pull himself up. When Casey's upper body was partly through the opening, Lexie reached over his shoulder to hold the window open for him until he, too, lay on the ground. They both lay in the snow for a moment, but then, at the same time, they got up and started running. They did not stop until they got to the street lamp in front of Lexie's house. Lexie leaned against the lamppost and Casey, bent at the waist, hands on his knees, tried to catch his breath.

"What's going on, now?" asked Lexie.
"What do you mean?"
"Take a look." Lexie pointed down Sandy Point Road toward Salt Marsh Bridge.

There were flashing blue lights, familiar to Casey. It was a police cruiser stopped at the intersection. But, within seconds, the blue lights stopped flashing.

"He's going away," said Casey.

At that moment, an earsplitting explosion startled Casey and Lexie. They looked toward the Samuelson house and it was on fire. Pieces of wood dropped out of the sky only a few feet away from where they stood. A rancid odor of hot, soot-filled smoke enveloped them. For just a few seconds. Casey grabbed Lexie's arm and they both ran for cover to Lexie's front porch where they stood in awe of the huge bonfire that was consuming the Samuelson house. Flames lit up the neighborhood. Lights came on in Lexie's house. Lexie's father came running out.

"Call 911," he hollered back into the house. "The Samuelson's house is on fire."

"Dad," shouted Lexie. "Over here."

"What now. What have you done?" asked Mr. Wentworth.

"What have we done?" asked Lexie. "What do you think we did?"

"Where have you been? What are you doing out at this hour?"

"Jake blew up the house. He thought we were in it. We were, for a while. He's got the coins," said Casey.

As Casey stopped talking, the police cruiser they saw earlier pulled up to them. A policeman got out and approached them.

"Hello, Joe," said Mr. Wentworth. The Fire Department is on the way,"

"I know. I called in, too. Do you know anything about this?"

"Jake Colby did it," said Lexie. "Didn't you stop him at the bridge?"

"Jake Colby? No, I haven't seen him. I stopped someone else, a man headed for work in the city. He was driving a little fast, so I told him to slow down."

"How long were you there, at the bridge?" asked Mr. Wentworth.

"At least half an hour."

"You didn't see Jake Colby?" asked Casey. "He must have gone by you."

" I know Jake Colby's car. He didn't go by me."

"You've got to find him. He must be still up there," said Lexie pointing to the Samuelson's house.

"He's got two bags filled with gold coins," said Casey. "He tried to kill us. He tied us up in the cellar. He thought we'd blow up with the house,"

The policeman ran to his cruiser and radioed to the police station calling for an All Points Bulletin on Jake. He returned to the group.

"If Jake didn't cross the bridge, he's got to be up here somewhere, probably at the Point," said Joe.

"Dad, can we take a ride up to the top to Sandy Point?" asked Lexie.

"Jake's car must be up there," said Casey. "There's no where else to go."

"You two go. I'm going to call your parents," said Mr. Wentworth to Casey.

Casey and Lexie got into the back seat of the cruiser. For a brief moment, Casey remembered the last time he rode in a cruiser. It was summer then, a few years ago. This time he felt the welcome warmth of the cruiser's heater and he was more conscious of the smell of this one, of old leather. This cruiser was older. In the dark, he could feel patches on the leather seats, but the power of the engine was unmistakably the same. They passed the Samuelson's house and Casey and Lexie looked back and saw the red glow in the sky. They looked back at each other. Neither spoke. As the cruiser approached Sandy Point, Casey spotted a car just out of range of the light from the street lamp. In the light from the cruiser's headlights, Casey recognized Jake's car.

13

Jake is Found

"**T**here it is," shouted Casey.

Jake's car was parked at Sandy Point facing down Sandy Point Road. The policeman turned the cruiser around and pulled up behind it, got out and opened the cruiser door to let Casey and Lexie out. The cold air, in stark contrast to the heat of the cruiser, sent shivers up Casey's spine. Lexie came close to him partly for warmth and partly in fear that they might find another dead body in the car. Casey felt the firm grip of Lexie's hand on his arm. Together they approached the back of Jake's station wagon. The policeman cautiously approached the driver's side of Jake's car and Casey and Lexie stayed in the back. The cruiser's head-lights lit up the back of Jake's car, but left dark shadows inside the station wagon.

"Nothing here," said Joe Thompson. Then, he directed his flashlight into the back of the station wagon.

"There's the blanket, the one Jake used to wrap Dorothy in," said Lexie.

"There's no sign of him here," said the policeman.

"He couldn't have walked home," said Casey.

"There's only one place he could be," said Lexie. "He must be in the house."

"Look there," said Casey. He pointed down Sandy Point Road where flashing red lights appeared.

"The fire engines are down there. Let's go back," said Joe Thompson. "They'll have to know about this, to try to find a body."

Casey took Lexie's arm and whispered "Want to walk back?"

"Sure."

Casey turned to Joe Thompson and said, "If it's OK with you, we'd like to walk back."

"No problem," said Joe. "Just don't get sidetracked on the way."

"We won't."

They watched Joe Thompson drive away and they were left in the soft light of the street lamp. From that point they had a clear view of the fire at the Samuelson house. After the initial explosion, the house was enveloped in a blaze that shot hundreds of feet into the night sky. Without thinking, Casey took Lexie's hand in his and pointed toward the house as another explosion with a sound like muffled thunder created another burst of flame that shot skyward.

"Another gas tank blew," said Casey.

It was like watching a fireworks display as flaming pieces of wood and bright orange flames shot into the sky. Sparks and flaming debris, carried by the offshore breeze, blew over Casey and Lexie's heads. As they stood there, drafts of warm air blew over them carrying billows of acrid smelling smoke. Then, as quickly as the flames appeared, they disappeared as the firemen worked their magic to bring the fire under control.

"Why did you want to walk back?" asked Lexie. She held his arm and moved closer as the breeze from the ocean blew cold once again. She shivered and Casey put his right arm around her and pulled her closer. Together, they walked toward Lexie's house.

"I guess this deal is all over now, except for cleaning up the mess," said Casey. He sounded tentative and sad. "I just want to say I'm sorry, again, that I got you into this. You could have been killed."

"I know. But, you saved me, didn't you? If you hadn't tied me up like that, we'd both be dead."

"Maybe so, but if I hadn't tried to cover.up all this the police could have done their thing."

"It was exciting, though, wasn't it?"

"Yeah, that's for sure."

"So, what happens now? Are you ever going to ask me out again? There are still lots of houses we haven't broken into."

"Do you want me to?"

"What? Break into more houses?"

"No, I mean, ask you out."

"Do I have to draw you a picture?"

Casey and Lexie walked by the fire engines and stood for a moment in awe at the work being done on the Samuelson house. They continued and paused under the street lamp at Lexie's house. They looked into each other's eyes and Casey said, "We'd better go inside."

As Lexie opened her front door, Casey's parents and his sister, Kathy, drove up and pulled into the Wentworth's driveway.

Lexie's parents were watching the fire through their living room window and saw the Millers drive in. Mr. Wentworth greeted them as they stepped onto the porch.

"Hi, Daddy," said Lexie.

"You may not believe any of this," said Mr. Wentworth. He put his arm around Mr. Miller's shoulder and guided him into the living room.

"This is getting to be a habit. What's going on now?" asked Mr. Miller.

"Jake Colby may be in the house," said Lexie.

"You think he got burned up in the fire?" asked Kathy. "Did you do it?"

"Never mind that," said Mr. Miller.

"Darn, I never have any fun."

Casey told the story of the night's activities as the rest of the group looked on in disbelief.

"Whatever possessed you to go into the Samuelson house?" asked Mrs. Miller.

"You've known about the coins for a long time, haven't you?" asked Mr. Wentworth. He directed his question at Lexie, but knew that Casey was more likely to be at the bottom of it all. Before Lexie could answer, Kathy broke into the conversation.

"Why did you lie to us?" asked Kathy.

"I didn't lie. I just didn't tell you about them?"

"But, why?" asked Mrs. Miller.

"Well, I thought there might be a reward. If someone else found them before us, we'd lose out."

"And you went along with this?" asked Mr. Wentworth pointing to Lexie.

"Sure. Neither one of us thought it would end up like this."

"We found the coins," said Casey.

"We broke the code," said Lexie.

"Lexie did," said Casey. He saw Lexie smile.

"We both did," insisted Lexie.

"Where are they?" asked Mr. Miller.

"Jake's got them," said Casey. "He tied us up and took the coins."

"I'll say it again. You sure know how to treat a girl on a date," said Kathy.

"You were tied up?" asked Mrs. Miller. "Where?"

"In Samuelson's cellar."

Mr. and Mrs. Miller looked at Kathy and said nothing. They didn't have to.

"We need a time out from all this. Let's go out on the porch. We can see the fire better from there," said Mrs. Wentworth.

No other words were spoken. The group marched out to the porch and stood silently watching the firemen pull back their hoses. By now, a small crowd of onlookers was gathered at the scene.

"Looks like it's almost over," said Mrs. Wentworth.

"They'll probably be there for the rest of the night to make sure it doesn't flare up again," said Mr. Miller.

"You're right about that," said Mr. Wentworth.

Thirty minutes later the fire was essentially out. They watched as one of the fire engines retreated with its red lights flashing, disappearing down Sandy Point Road. The other stayed. The firemen would spend another half hour soaking the charred hulk of the Samuelson house to make sure no hidden sparks would set it off again. Another cadre of six people arrived in two official-looking cars. Chief Fallon was with them. They gathered under the street lamp in front of Lexie's house and, after receiving instructions from The Chief, they dispersed and headed toward the Samuelson house. Chief Fallon approached the Wentworth's porch, but stopped momentarily to have a brief conversation with Joe Thompson. Joe got into his cruiser, turned around and drove back up Sandy Point Road. The Chief walked slowly up the steps with his eyes trained on Casey and Lexie. Casey could tell he was not pleased.

"We need to talk," said the Chief. He pointed to Casey, then to Lexie.

"Let's go in the house," said Mr. Wentworth. "It's too cold out here. Maybe these two detectives will fill us in."

"I can hardly wait," said Kathy. "Why can't I get dates like this?"

The group assembled in the Wentworth's living room. Mrs. Wentworth brought mugs of hot chocolate. "I thought this would be better than coffee at this hour."

Casey looked at the clock on the mantle. It was four fifteen. Up until now Casey had not felt tired, but as he relaxed in the comfort of the Wentworth's couch, his energy began to fade. He looked across the room at Lexie who was sitting on a piano bench. She smiled, but she looked tired.

"Now, Mr. Miller, I mean you, Casey," said The Chief. "How did you end up in the Samuelson house?"

"I just thought the coins would be there. I didn't know we'd run into Jake."

"What coins?" asked The Chief.

"Oliver Colby, in the letter I told you about, said he left some coins for his relatives. Something about his being worried that he'd be ruined if the word got out about what they did with Anne Robertson."

"That was a hundred years ago. You still haven't answered my question."

"It was just a guess," said Lexie. "We found ten old coins in Dorothy Moorehead's house. We were after the letter she had and Casey found the coins."

"There were only ten of them. The letter said there was more. Lots more," said Casey

"Four hundred and ninety, to be exact," said Lexie.

"Dorothy's house was trashed. I figured Jake must have been looking for them. Why else would he have done what he did?" Casey paused as if he was looking for an answer from the group, but all looked bewildered.

"Joe Thompson told me that you found Jake's car," said The Chief. "I sent him back up there to stand guard. We'll have to sort out these details later. I want you in the station at eleven today."

"So, where is Jake?" asked Mrs. Wentworth.

"We think he was in the house when it exploded," said Lexie.

"My men will begin searching the area after the firemen finish. In the meantime, tell me why I shouldn't arrest you for breaking and entering."

"We didn't take anything. The house was boarded up and I thought we could find the coins before Jake took off."

"What about all the other houses. You broke into Jake's house, you broke into Dorothy Moorehead's and now the Samuelson's. Whose house is next?"

"There won't be anymore," said Casey.

"Is that a promise?" asked Kathy. "What do you say, Lexie?"

"That's enough, Kath," said Mr. Miller.

"What about the coins?" asked The Chief.

"We found them in the cellar. That's when Jake caught us and we got tied up."

Mrs. Miller looked at Mrs. Wentworth in disbelief.

"Jake made Casey tie me up," said Lexie. "But Casey was really smart. He tied me up with a knot that came undone really easy. That's how we got out of the house after Jake left us. Jake's got the coins, two leather bags full."

The Wentworth's doorbell rang. Mr. Wentworth went to the front door.

"Chief, it's for you," he said. "It's Joe Thompson. Come in, Joe."

"What's up?" asked The Chief.

"They found Jake. He's dead."

The group gasped. Casey looked at Lexie. She was not smiling. He got up off the couch and went over to sit next to her.

"Where?" asked The Chief.

"He must have been standing on the back porch when the explosion hit. He was thrown into the back yard. A fireman found him laying face down in the snow with two leather bags of coins beside him. It was so dark out there nobody noticed him until the cleanup crew put up some floodlights."

"They didn't move him, did they?" asked The Chief.

"No, he's still there."

"Go back and find Andy Chang. He came with me. Tell him to take charge and secure the area. Bill Summers is there, too. He's a photographer. Have him take pictures and then you take custody of the two bags. Call for a tow truck to take Jake's car back to the station. Don't let anyone touch it."

After Joe Thompson left, The Chief spoke in somber tones. "You know, I haven't had anything like this happen since I came on the force.

Casey Miller moves into town and the next thing I know I've got a skeleton in the library, two bodies and a house blown up. Can I use your phone? I need to wake up the coroner."

Casey and Lexie sat close together. Both of them listened as The Chief made his phone call.

After he hung up, The Chief turned to the group and, with a smile on his face, spoke to Casey and Lexie. "I think we've had enough for one night. I'll see you at station at eleven today. I'll need a statement from both of you. You won't need a lawyer. I just want to put the pieces of this puzzle together."

All of the family members nodded their agreement.

"We'll be there," said Mr. Miller. "See you then."

After Chief Fallon left, the group just looked at each other, then all eyes turned to Casey.

"What?" asked Casey.

"What do you mean, what?" asked Kathy.

"Never mind. It's time to go home," said Mrs. Miller.

"See you later, Lexie," said Casey. "Too bad about the coins. I was hoping we'd get a reward."

"Thanks, Casey. See you at the station."

When Casey got home, he was too exhausted to talk to his parents or Kathy. He went straight up to his room. But, as hard as he tried, he could not relax. He lay awake for an hour recounting every step in this incredible adventure.

✱   ✱   ✱

At eleven in the morning Casey and his parents and Kathy arrived at the police station. The Wentworths arrived at the same time and all of them were escorted into Chief Fallon's office by a policeman.

"Please, have a seat," said The Chief. "I'm sorry we don't have any coffee and Danish. We've been pretty busy here this morning."

Casey's parents and the Wentworths sat in folding chairs. They left seats in a leather couch for Casey and Lexie. Casey supposed it was to help Lexie and him relax, but it wasn't working. The office was too warm for Casey. He felt like the walls were closing in and he felt like he had a lump in his throat. His eyes felt like they had sand in them from lack of sleep. His stomach was churning, partly from hunger, but mostly from fear. He had spent a restless night. He had spent the whole Summer and Fall avoiding contact with anyone who would possibly bring up the Shorewood affair. And now he was in the exact place he was trying to avoid. As he looked around the room, he could only think of one saying he had heard often in Shorewood, 'what comes around, comes around.' He looked at Lexie and saw that she was much more relaxed. She smiled her usual smile, but that didn't help Casey.

"Are you all right, Casey?" asked The Chief.

Casey's stuttered. "I, I, I'm OK."

"Relax," said The Chief. "This isn't going to hurt."

That was easy enough for him to say and it made Casey more nervous. The sooner he got out of there, the better.

"Before we begin, Casey, you must be famous. Are you public enemy number one, or what?"

"What do you mean?" Casey began to feel sick to his stomach.

"I just got this long report by FAX in from Shorewood about you." He held up several sheets of paper.

Casey was terrified. He felt like running, but he could only sit in utter silence. He felt a bead of sweat run down his back.

"What's that, Chief?" asked Mrs. Miller.

"A friend of yours, Robert Keith walked into the Shorewood station yesterday and told the real story about the death of William Keith, his brother. Two other boys were with him. Do you know a Rosario Germano and a Donny Nabors?"

"Y-Y-Yes," stammered Casey.

"We know them," said Kathy. "They're part of that evil Sandbox gang."

"That's enough," said Mr. Miller. "Chief, we know those boys. What's this all about?"

"It says here that the Shorewood police closed their murder investigation. A boy named William Keith died under suspicious circumstances this past summer."

"The Keith's lived across the street from us in Shorewood," said Mrs. Miller. "It was a terrible thing, Billy's death."

"Anyway, Robert cleared a few things up. The police, at one time, wanted to know about Casey's involvement. In here it says something about a Sandbox Gang. They questioned everyone who was a friend of William Keith."

"We didn't know that Casey was a suspect," said Mr. Miller. "He was interviewed by the police."

"He wasn't a suspect. Just routine follow-up stuff. It was interesting, though. When Robert walked in the coroner had already submitted his report, that William died from a fall and not by anyone's hand. But, those boys will have to appear in Juvenile Court about the break-in. It was nice of the police up there to send me a report."

"They know we moved here," said Mr. Miller. "I made sure of that before we left."

Casey was dumfounded. He temporarily forgot about the matter at hand. It was like a great weight lifted from his shoulders. He looked at Lexie. She was grinning now.

"Oh, Casey. How good you must feel?"

"It feels great."

"What's that all about?" asked Kathy.

"The Grinch is dead, that's all," said Casey.

"Mom, what's Casey talking about?"

"I guess we'll have to wait for that. What about the statement?" asked Mrs. Miller.

"I'm going to take Casey and Lexie into another room and ask some questions and we'll record the session. You are welcome to sit in. This is not going to incriminate Casey or Lexie or anything like that. We just need pieces of the puzzle. Before we do, though, I want you to know that we hired a private detective to look into the backgrounds of Dorothy Moorehead and Jake Colby. It's a little out of the ordinary, but, we just don't have the staff with the time to do something like that. I expect his report later today. He started right after you first told me about all this."

Casey and Lexie spent the next three hours answering detailed questions about their involvement with the Anne Robertson case and events leading up to the deaths of Dorothy Moorehead and Jake Colby. Their parents and Kathy were awestruck by what they heard. When finished, both were totally exhausted from the stress of the questioning and the lack of sleep.

"Thank you. You two have been most helpful," said The Chief. "I'll never understand what made you push on with this thing, but you can keep that to yourselves. I can't think of any more reasons why you should have to come back, but who knows."

"Thanks," said Casey. "And thanks for telling me about Bobby Keith."

When Casey stepped outside, he stood on the steps of the police station and took deep breaths. He was proud of himself for being loyal to Bobby, but it disturbed him that he would participate in a cover-up like that in the first place. He seriously doubted that something like that would ever happen again. He had put himself in a trap and it had affected everyone around him, especially Lexie. Now, he was free.

"Want to go to the Malt Shop?" asked Casey.

"Sure," answered Lexie.

"Can I go, too?" asked Kathy. "You guys were great in there."

"Sure, you can come," said Casey.

"You look tired. Come home and take a nap," said Mrs. Miller.

"Are you tired, Lexie?"

"Not me."

"All right, we'll drop you there on the way home," said Mrs. Miller.

It was one hour after they left the police station when The Chief got his report from the detective.

Chief Fallon's Notes
The Family of Oliver Colby

Oliver Colby
b. 1819
d. 1904
1877 marr. Sarah Hennessey
b. 1853
d. 1917

Matilda Colby	Andrew Colby
b. 1879	b. 1878
d. 1904 (in childbirth)	d. 1919 (killed, WWI)
1903 marr. Nathaniel Hogarth	1902 marr. Ida Swanson

Henrietta Hogarth	Harold Colby
b. 1904	b. 1903
d. 1972	d. 1969
1925 marr. Thomas Anderson	1939 marr. Mary Swift

Elizabeth Anderson	Jacob Colby
b. 1927	b. 1941
d. 1966	d. 1998
1946 marr. Henry Amesbury	Never married

Julie Amesbury
b. 1945

1965 marr. Edward Miller

14

More Revelations

Casey was awakened by the ringing of the telephone downstairs. Through glazed eyes he glanced at his clock. It was seven forty-five. It took him several seconds to realize it was Sunday morning. He wondered who would be calling at this hour. He looked out his bedroom window and saw that it was a dreary, foggy day. A warm front was moving Northeasterly and when this happened fog as thick as pea soup covered the area. A front like this could remain over Elm Grove for several days with temperatures hovering at thirty-eight to forty degrees. The snow throughout the area would melt away. However, this was not the end of Winter by any stretch of imagination. Snow storms were expected at any time in the next three months, even into March. Out of curiosity, Casey went to the top of the stairs, but his mother had talked briefly on the phone and had already hung up. Casey shrugged his shoulders and returned to bed and pulled the covers over his head.

*   *   *

The phone call was from The Chief.

"I apologize for calling so early, but I have some startling news and I'm just busting a gut to tell you," said The Chief. "I need to come over right away. Your whole family will be interested in this."

"We'll be here."

"See you in about an hour."

"Casey! Kathy! Wake up," hollered Mrs. Miller.

"What's going on?" asked Mr. Miller. He shouted from the living room from his usual perch in his astronaut seat. He was still in pajamas and bathrobe.

"Chief Fallon is coming over. He's got something to tell us."

"I'll go change," said Mr. Miller.

"Wake up Casey and Kathy," hollered Mrs. Miller.

"I'll get them up," said Mr. Miller.

"I'll make some more coffee," said Mrs. Miller.

Mr. Miller knocked on Casey's door, then Kathy's.

"Time to get up, kids. Let's go." He pounded more heavily on each door.

Casey curled up more tightly than before. He did not like to be awakened out of a dead sleep, but when his door opened and his father looked at him with the look that meant business, he roused himself, rubbed his eyes and trudged into the bathroom. On the way, he heard groans coming from Kathy's room. She, too, was fighting waking up. Casey splashed cold water on his face, brushed his teeth and finished what he had to do in the bathroom and passed Kathy on the way back into his room.

"What have you done, now? " asked Kathy.

"Nothing, Kath, nothing."

Casey closed the door to his room and got dressed. He could smell a rich odor of hot chocolate brewing mixed with the aroma of coffee as he descended the stairs. He turned around and saw his father coming down the stairs behind him, fully dressed now in corduroy pants, a green plaid flannel shirt and slippers on his feet. When Casey and his father met at the door to the kitchen, Casey stepped aside.

"After you, Dad," said Casey in a polite tone of voice.

"Oh, oh. What now?" said Mr. Miller.

"There's nothing that I know of," said Mrs. Miller. "Chief Fallon sounded really excited about something. He should be here any minute."

"I'm hungry," said Kathy as she came into the kitchen.

"There's hot chocolate and Danish on the table. Some of it is for The Chief so don't go wild," said Mrs. Miller.

Moments later the front door bell rang. Kathy opened the door and let The Chief in.

"How about some coffee, Chief," said Mr. Miller.

"That will be fine."

"What brings you here?" asked Mrs. Miller. "You sounded excited and mysterious on the phone."

"I think I've got some great news. Can we go into the living room?"

The group settled down in the living room and The Chief began his explanation of his good news.

"When the letters were found, I had a chance to read them carefully several times, then I remembered that the Historical Society owned this house and that you bought it from them. I asked Gloria Morgan, my secretary, to contact someone in the Historical Society to look into the archives for any information they had about Oliver Colby and your house. I was curious because of a few things that came up later. The discovery of the coins is one of those things. I wanted to find out who Oliver's legal heirs may be. My private detective found the answer."

"What's going to happen to the coins?" asked Casey. "Is there any reward?"

"There's no reward, but I think what I have to tell you is more important."

"Gloria's friend in the Historical Society came up with a startling revelation. She discovered an old manuscript that Oliver Colby's grandniece put together. I don't have it with me, but I took some notes."

The Chief brought out a yellow legal pad and began reading his notes.

This is the Colby family tree dating back several hundred years. Starting with Oliver, he was born in 1819. He married late. He was fifty-eight when he married Sarah Hennessey, who was age twenty-four, in 1877. They had a son, Andrew, born in 1878 and a daughter, Matilda born in 1879. Andrew married Ida Swanson in 1902. They had a son named Harold in 1903. Tragically, Andrew died in World War I. Harold married Mary Swift in 1939. They had only one child, Jacob in 1941.

"Jake?" asked Casey.

"Right," answered The Chief. "Oliver died in 1904 at age 85. His wife died one year later. Here comes the interesting part. Matilda married a man named Nathaniel Hogarth. Tragically, she died giving birth to a daughter in 1904. The daughter was named Henrietta. But, the record stopped there. My private detective took it from there and dug up some birth records in the county archives. Henrietta married Thomas Anderson and they had a daughter named Elizabeth. Elizabeth married Henry Amesbury."

"Elizabeth Amesbury?" asked Mrs. Miller. "That was my mother."

"Yes. It looks like you may be an heir to the Colby estate."

"When I was growing up, I asked my mother about my grandparents, but she never gave me a straight answer."

"It isn't so strange. Not too many people want to admit that they are related to Oliver Colby. He was a mean rascal or, at least that's what the history says of him."

"It's been so long ago and how weird it is that I ended up in my family's house."

"Does that mean she gets the coins?" asked Casey.

"You're pretty interested in those coins, aren't you? Well, as far as I know the coins are all that's left in the estate. The courts will have to decide, but it's clear that they were Oliver's coins, even though he got them under suspicious circumstances. There's no way to prove that he committed a crime. The letters provide a convincing paper trail, proving that he gave the coins to Samuelson. We'll never know why or how Samuelson kept them, but one thing is sure, they must be the same coins since they were found in his house."

"What about Pritchard, Oliver's partner?"

"Gloria traced Jason Pritchard's family, too. He died in 1951. He never married so there is no one to claim in the name of the partnership."

"What about Jonathan?" asked Lexie.

"Jonathan was the son of a distant cousin. Jonathan's parents died and Jason and his wife took Jonathan in. Jason and his wife had no children of their own. Jonathan died in 1951. He never married."

"And Jake? Where does he fit in?" asked Mrs. Miller.

"I hope you're ready for this. Jake was your cousin. He never married. There are no heirs on his side of the family. It looks like you're the only surviving heir. You may get it all, or what's left after the IRS has its way."

"How did Dorothy Moorehead end up with some of the coins?" asked Lexie.

"I've got that, too. James Samuelson and Jason Pritchard were good friends. In fact, both of their houses, yours and his, were built with the same plans. It doesn't prove anything, but it would explain a couple of things. First, Samuelson handled the legal work for the partnership. He may have known about Anne's death and what Oliver and Jason did with her. He could have kept the coins as blackmail. The reason we think that is that his son, Marcus left ten coins to his daughter, Penelope, long before Oliver or Jason died. Also, the fact that both Oliver and Jason wrote their letters speaks volumes about the trust they had for each other. Samuelson had plenty of opportunities to play one off the other."

"What does that have to do with Dorothy?" asked Mr. Wentworth.

"Penelope married Robert Bates. They had a daughter, Dorothy, who married Albert Moorehead."

"So, that's it. We could write a book about this," said Mrs. Wentworth.

"And you could illustrate it, Mom," said Lexie.

"Are the coins very valuable?" asked Kathy.

"That's another thing I did. I had a professional coin collector come in to look at the coins. I had to know what to do with them. I'm no expert on coins, but if they were valuable, I didn't want them in the station. He says they are very rare. The coins should have been part of a large shipment that came out of the San Francisco mint in 1857. Somehow, Oliver Colby was paid under the table for doing someone a favor and he got some of the coins. There was a rumor that Oliver got an extra kickback when he sold part of Moss Island. The coins weren't as valuable then as they are now."

"How valuable are they?" interrupted Kathy.

"I'm getting to that."

"A large gold shipment was on the SS Central America and that ship sank on the way to New York. That was in 1857. The peculiar thing about the coins you found is that they are of such high quality. Are you ready for what they're worth? Hang onto your seat. Our professional says that the whole collection is worth over four million dollars. There are four hundred and sixty-four coins in the bags. It looks like Mr. Samuelson dipped into them."

Casey looked at his family. They were struck dumb by the news.

"This is a joke, right?" said Casey. "Four million?"

"It's no joke. Again, it's up to a judge to decide, but legally, I think you stand to get quite a bundle."

"Will we get the coins or what they are worth in cash?" asked Kathy. "I like the wrinkly, green stuff better."

"That I don't know. Once the IRS accepts the valuation, it could go either way. I don't see any reason why they wouldn't give you the coins. I think the way it works is that you get all the coins, then you have to pay the tax on the value they put on them. You'll need cash for that. I have a feeling that coin traders will be parked on your doorstep as soon as word gets out. I've sworn Gloria and her friend to secrecy, but you know how that works."

"When will we know for sure?" asked Mr. Miller. "About getting the coins."

"It could take three months, six months or a year. It all depends on how soon the IRS gets and accepts a valuation of the coins. At the same time, since I've taken custody of the coins, I've petitioned the probate judge myself to have him determine who the rightful owner is. He has Oliver's letter and the documents from the archives. It should be a simple matter, but he has to check to see if everything is authentic."

"Where are the coins now? Where will they go?" asked Casey.

"They have been placed in a vault at the Elm Grove Federal Saving Bank. That's where they will stay and that's where the coins will be looked at, officially, that is."

"We can't thank you enough for the way you've handled all this," said Mrs. Miller.

"There's more to be done. The letters we have confirm that the skeleton we found is Anne Robertson, thanks to your son's handiwork."

"And Lexie. Don't forget Lexie. She was with me all the way. I wouldn't have done it alone."

"I won't forget. The town will be very grateful for this mystery being solved. I've got to get going. Congratulations. You may be millionaires. By the way, we won't need to tie up your cellar anymore. That part of the case is over."

∗   ∗   ∗

The search of the library, scheduled for January thirteenth, was delayed for three days due to a northeast storm. By the time the storm subsided, Elm Grove was reeling from severe damage. Along the coast, hundreds of summer cottages were reduced to matchwood. Electricity was cut off for three days because of power lines damaged from falling trees. At the storm's end, however, the town was transformed into a picturesque, serene New England landscape. School closings gave the children of Elm Grove an extra three-day holiday. Snowmen of all shapes and sizes popped up on front lawns all over town. The slopes at the Elm Grove Country Club were filled with squealing, happy children on sleds, skis, saucers, cardboard and anything else they could find to carry them down the hill. Men with snow plows did their work well. One day after the storm, neat drifts of snow lined the streets. None of the townspeople expected the chaos to come.

When Chief Fallon broke the news about the search of the library, a small cadre of newspaper and TV reporters were already in Elm Grove reporting on the Samuelson house fire, Dorothy and Jake's deaths and the storm damage. Dozens more descended on the town like a swarm of bees when word went out that a body was buried in the library. The Chief closed the library and cordoned it off. He then called a press conference in the high school assembly hall.

"I'm here to tell you that we are conducting an investigation into a tip from what I believe is a well-informed source that there might be the remains of a body buried in the basement of the library."

When pressed to reveal why he was doing this, The Chief told the inquisitive reporters that a tip came from an anonymous source. He withheld any reference to Ann Robertson, the two deaths or Casey and Lexie's involvement. Traffic on Old Country Lane was restricted to snowplows, police cars, and construction trucks. It took one whole day just to get equipment and personnel in place. A small army of volunteers with shovels kept the sidewalks cleared of snow while three men carefully dug up the cellar crawl space. There was no precedent for this in the entire history of the town.

At noon on the second day, in the unfinished part of the cellar, the workmen dug through a layer of clay-like soil and found the remains of a skeleton in sandy soil about four feet below the surface. The Chief surmised that Colby and Pritchard buried Anne in a shallow grave when the area was first dug out for the foundation. Later, possibly under orders from Jason Pritchard, the builders topped off the grave and unknowingly finished the job for Oliver and Jason.

The skeleton was placed in the morgue at the County Coroner's office where it remained for two days. From there, it was transported to the state forensic laboratory. Preliminary tests showed that the person was between the ages of fifteen and twenty, approximately five feet three inches tall with dark brown hair. A blow to the forehead was deemed to be the cause of death. The description could match Ann Robertson, but there were no dental records and no other evidence to link the skeleton with Colby and Pritchard. An examination of the grave revealed tiny shreds of a lightweight cloth. There was no jewelry or identification of any kind. It would take weeks to get a thorough analysis of the skeleton and how long the remains had been there.

Chief Fallon withheld the information about how he found out about the skeleton and why he ordered the search pending the results of the analysis by the forensic lab. He had to be sure that the skeleton was a hundred years old. The investigation of the library continued for two more days to see if any other clues linked to the skeleton could be found in the area No other clues were found. Finally, the investigation was closed. Police withdrew their guards and traffic returned to normal. The library was allowed to reopen while workmen filled the dirt back in and cleaned up the mess on the cellar floor. Fortunately, Rebecca Stone and a group of volunteers from the Friends of the Library, took over the running of the library.

*   *   *

The forensic lab confirmed the age of the skeleton. Chief Fallon then released copies of the Colby-Pritchard letters to the press. A committee comprising members of the town council and the Elm Grove Historical Society studied the evidence, conferred with The Chief and spoke with Casey and Lexie in private. The council declared officially that Anne Robertson was the skeleton and that the letters were authentic.

During the month that followed, Casey and Lexie spent virtually all of their free time trying to hide from probing reporters and cameramen. They were now celebrities in the town, but the excitement was wearing thin. Their pictures appeared in the local and city papers, news broadcasts chronicled their involvement in the case as an act of heroism and it seemed that every politician in the state wanted a picture taken with them. They had recapped the past events so many times in press interviews with town council members and other politicians from the state capitol that it became boring and tiresome.

The archives showed that the Robertson's were avid churchgoers. When the matter of identifying the skeleton was settled, members of the Episcopal Church came forward to offer a funeral service for Anne. The Miller's invited the Wentworths and The Chief to come for Sunday dinner before they went to the funeral. This was a time when Casey and Lexie could ask the questions that had been bothering them since the case broke open.

"Why did Oliver and Jason cover things up?" asked Casey. He was sitting at the Miller's dining room table with the Wentworths and his family.

"Oliver and Jason were pretty clear about that. Money and power are usually at the bottom of it," said Mr. Miller.

"I see it a lot in my work, in sales, and you can read about it every day in the newspaper or hear about it on TV. Money and power are what drives most everything these days. That's what Watergate was all about," said Mr. Wentworth. "That partnership had a bad reputation to begin with. Anne's death would have done them in."

"Some people just cannot be counted on to step forward and do the honest thing when they should. Unfortunately, it seems to be a way of life these days. Too many people, I'm afraid, think that anything is OK, until they get caught," said Mrs. Miller. "But, isn't it great that Bobby and the other boys did what was right in the end?"

"I didn't know what to do," said Casey, "about Bobby Keith, I mean. He put me in a tough spot. What should I have done?"

"That's a tough one to answer," said The Chief. "Remember, though, you had very little information to go on. Bobby painted a grim picture. Had he come forward like he should have, Bobby, probably, would have been put on probation for breaking into the lumber yard. He thought he might go to jail. None of the boys was responsible for Billy's death. No one was going to send the boys to jail. Bobby didn't trust anyone, even his mother and because of that you got trapped."

"It's easy for me, at my age, to say that you should have come forward and told someone, but that wouldn't be fair," said Mr. Miller. "I think I would have done the same thing you did, but I'm sure I would have tried to get Bobby to tell his mother."

"I didn't get the chance. We moved."

"So that's why you became such a grouch," said Kathy.

"I just didn't know what would happen if I told on Bobby."

"You could have told us," said Mrs. Miller.

"If it hadn't been for the Anne Robertson case, I would never have said anything, but I was ready once this thing cleared up. I was going to go to Shorewood to talk to Bobby. I was wrong to cover it up just like

Oliver and Jason. I made it worse when I didn't say anything about the coins."

"I know," said Lexie. "I went along with it, too."

"That part wasn't your fault. You tried to set me straight."

"We didn't know the whole story, especially about your promise to Bobby," said Mr. Miller. "We were worried about you and your connection with The Sandbox Gang You were pretty loyal to those people, that part is good, and we know how hard it is when you think you're ratting on your friends. Maybe you thought we wouldn't handle it right, your telling us about it."

"If I told you, you would have told everyone, including the police. Bobby was there. He told me what happened. He was afraid of being arrested. What about the newspapers? They said the police were investigating a possible murder."

"Our old friend, Gooseneck, told me about that," said The Chief. "There was an investigation. They do that in all cases, but the newspapers wrongly built that up."

"I'm glad it finally worked out for you," said Mrs. Wentworth. "How do you feel, now?"

"Like I weigh a hundred pounds lighter."

"They arrested Bobby and Rosie and Donny, didn't they?" asked Casey.

"Yes, all of them, but Hank Sullivan is going to help. When they go to court, he's going to recommend probation."

"Hank Sullivan," said Bob Wentworth. "You don't mean Gooseneck Sullivan."

"The same. He graduated with us from Elm Grove High."

Casey didn't know what to say. The most feared policeman in the city of Shorewood was one of his father's best friends. He looked at Lexie. She smiled

"Small world, isn't it?" said Mrs. Wentworth.

"I still don't know why Jake killed Dorothy. What's that all about?" asked Kathy.

"This gets even more complicated," said The Chief. "We found boxes of letters and old documents in Dorothy's house. Dorothy was a great-granddaughter of James Samuelson. She got the coins you found in her house from Penelope, as I said. Somehow, she found Jason's letter. She and her husband rented the Pritchard house, your house, when she first came to Elm Grove."

"So, that's why we didn't find it," said Lexie.

"We know now, from a diary that Dorothy kept, that Dorothy and her husband, who died shortly after they got here, were involved in a questionable real estate deal in Ohio. That's why they moved. It was Dorothy's husband who cornered Jake one day, told him about the Colby-Pritchard cover-up and threatened to reveal the secret to the town, but they had no idea there were any coins around. He sold Jake on the idea that Jake would be ruined in the town that he would lose his job and he would have to move away. Dorothy and her husband thought Jake fell for it, but Jake was clever, too. There were letters found in his house, from his mother, confirming that he knew about the letter in your cellar. He needed time to get it, so, he bided his time, paying them off to keep quiet until he could get the letter out of our cellar, but you got there first."

"I don't understand," said Casey. "Did Jake know about the coins?"

"Yes, his mother went into a nursing home while Jake was away. She had no money and, probably, too sick to break the code or hire a lawyer. So, she hoped Jake would be able to take care of it. Unfortunately, she had to sell this house to pay for her nursing home and she couldn't recover the letter from the cellar."

"She probably didn't trust anyone. She was alone, wasn't she? That's what the Historical Society told us."

"Blackmail over something that happened a hundred years ago?" asked Mrs. Miller.

"I guess Dorothy and her husband thought it was, but to Jake it was just buying time. Dorothy's husband must have been a great salesman, but he wasn't greedy. He got Jake to agree to paying him something every month, just enough so that Jake wouldn't quit on the idea. But, as I said, Jake was the clever one. When Dorothy's husband died, Dorothy took over and things went well for a while."

"Then what happened," asked Kathy. "This sounds great."

"It was all right until Casey and Lexie started to look into the pieces of the puzzle."

"Jake knew all along that there was a letter in our house, but he took too long to get it," said Casey. "He told us."

"So, he got the letter and it would prove that he was the rightful heir, if he could find the coins. Jake must have discovered that Dorothy was a Samuelson, so now the stakes got a little higher. He must have thought Dorothy had all of the coins, but she only got a few of them."

"Ten, to be exact," said Lexie.

"At some point, Jake must have blurted out to her that there were more coins or maybe he threatened to expose Dorothy as a blackmailer if she didn't hand them over. But, in her diary, we know that she had no idea there were so many. They argued and it got so heated that Jake struck Dorothy and she died, we think, after falling against Jake's fireplace. The autopsy showed that she died from a blow to the back of her head and there were hair fibers found at Jake's house and on the blanket he wrapped her in. We wouldn't have looked there at all if Casey and Lexie hadn't told us about their argument."

"And it didn't stop there, did it?" asked Kathy.

"He probably went off the deep end when he found out that Casey and Lexie found Oliver's letter. He really got desperate. And then when his scheme to get rid of Dorothy's body failed, he was in real trouble. Somehow, he realized that there was only one other place to go to look for the coins."

"Samuelson's house," said Lexie.

"Right."

"He didn't know where the coins were hidden," said Casey.

"We found them before he did," said Lexie.

"With you out of the way, he might have gotten away with it."

"If Casey and Lexie hadn't found Dorothy and figured out where the coins were he would have," said Mrs. Miller.

"Yes, Casey and Lexie were pains in the neck. They just wouldn't go away. It's clear that Dorothy and Jake came to the same conclusion that Casey and Lexie did, about the whereabouts of the coins."

"We found the scrap of paper. Dorothy broke the code," said Casey.

"But, Jake hadn't," said The Chief. "When Jake went into the Samuelson house, he never expected that Casey and Lexie would show up there so soon. It was in the middle of the night, after all. He just wanted to get the coins. If everything worked out for him, he could have gone home a wealthy man, cooled it for a while. Then he could do whatever he wanted. He didn't realize that Dorothy kept her diary about him. It would have been destroyed in the fire he planned. He would be a free man today, if Casey and Lexie hadn't barged in."

"We're very proud of what you did," said Mrs. Miller.

"And you, Lexie, you deserve a medal for going along with Casey," said Mr. Miller.

"It was fun," said Lexie.

"We have to get going," said Mrs. Miller. "We told Mr. Hanley we'd be at the funeral parlor at one-thirty."

"I'll help clear the dishes," said Lexie.

"You've done enough. Kathy and I will take care of it. We'll just stack them and clean up when we get back."

"Why are we stopping there, the funeral isn't until two?" said Kathy.

"A little unfinished business," said Mr. Miller.

✴   ✴   ✴

At one-thirty the Millers and the Wentworths walked into Hanley's Funeral Parlor. Casey hated funeral parlors. He hated the pungent odor of flowers and there was always a faint smell of incense or something they used to cover up other smells. He had been to three funerals before this and he never could make any sense out of them. Today, it was different. Somehow, Anne Robertson deserved this. He knew Anne wouldn't know about it, of course, but, for the town's sake it was a good idea to bury someone correctly. She did not deserve to be treated the way she had been by Oliver Colby and Jason Pritchard. This was a good way to correct a terrible wrong. It would not erase what two selfish men did almost a hundred years ago, but it would, at least, show that someone cared.

Casey reached out to hold Lexie's hand as they moved together toward the closed casket. Many of the flowers donated by caring people had been removed and the casket was ready to be taken out to a waiting hearse. Casey's mother and father came up behind them and Mrs. Miller took something out of her purse. She handed it to Casey. It was the ring she bought. He turned it over in his hand until he could read the inscription. It was still there, JMP to AR 3/98. He handed it to Lexie. He took the other ring out of his pocket.

"Are you sure you want to do this, Mom?"

"I'm sure. I wouldn't feel right wearing the ring, especially if I had to take the inscription off. It belongs with Anne. I'm pleased that you thought about giving your ring first. It's a nice thing to do."

At that moment, Mr. Hanley entered the room. "Good afternoon," he said. "I'm James Hanley. I understand you have a special request."

"Yes, we do," said Casey. "We'd like these rings put in the casket to go with Anne Robertson."

"Certainly, but I'm afraid you will have to leave while I do it."

"We don't want to watch," said Lexie.

No one in the room had any need to see Anne's remains. Casey, especially, preferred to remember Anne from her yearbook picture.

Later that afternoon, a large gathering of people, braving the cold, stood in the snow by Anne's grave site. A brisk ice cold breeze blew in from the southeast across the North River and over the salt flats to the Woodlawn Cemetery. Brief words were spoken by Reverend Hill, the Episcopal Church minister and the group dispersed. Anne Robertson, with the rings, was finally laid to rest and so was Casey's burden.

Epilogue

*C*asey and Lexie returned to school after the February vacation. The sounds of his schoolmates, the heat in the hallways and the general chilly atmosphere of the students toward them hadn't changed. They went to their classes as usual. When they were together in their third period English class, a blaring list of announcements came over the loudspeaker from the Principal's office. For the most part, the announcements were the ordinary ones they heard throughout the school year. The last, however, was different.

"Fourth and fifth periods are canceled. All students will report to the auditorium at two fifteen." The Principal's announcement was brief and without explanation.

After class, Casey and Lexie walked together downstairs to their closets, put away their books and went to the auditorium. When they returned to the hallway, no one was there.

"Looks like everyone's in the auditorium," said Lexie.

When they arrived, the entire student body was there and strangely silent. Usually, before an assembly started, everyone would be babbling and the principal would have to scream into a microphone to quiet them down. Casey made a move toward two empty seats in a back row, but a boy in the first seat blocked him and shook his head. Lexie grabbed his hand and motioned to two seats farther down the aisle. When she tried to lead the way to the seats, a girl on the end blocked them, too.

"This is great," said Casey. "What are we supposed to do, sit on the floor?"

"Let's go," said Lexie. "We don't need this."

Lexie took Casey's hand and the two walked back to the exit. Two of the largest male students in the school were stationed at the door to prevent their leaving. Suddenly, a voice from the stage, booming over the loudspeaker, called to them.

"Casey Miller and Alexandra Wentworth. Come to the stage." It was the President of the Student Council, Angela Jameson.

"Now what?" asked Casey.

"What does she think she's doing?" asked Lexie.

"Casey and Lexie, come up here," shouted the voice from the stage.

The two burly students walked down the aisle toward them. They had nowhere to go, except toward the stage. Angela came over and beckoned to them to join her. She reached out to take Lexie's hand. Lexie took her hand and went up the stairs with Casey behind her. As soon as both were on the stage, the audience of students and teachers erupted with a standing ovation. Angela opened her arms and gave Lexie a hug, then did the same to Casey. From offstage, Chief Fallon, members of the Town Council and school administrators and staff marched onto the stage and surrounded Casey and Lexie and the applause continued.

"What's wrong?" asked Casey. "What's going on?"

"It's all for you," said The Chief.

Everyone stepped back and a curtain at the back of the stage opened to reveal a huge flat cake large enough to feed the entire school and all the guests. The cake was inscribed with the words, "Casey and Lexie, Elm Grove's Heroes." The Wentworths and the Millers stood by the cake.

For the next hour and a half, several speakers praised Casey's and Lexie's exploits, their incredible persistence, their brilliance in uncovering the secrets of the hundred-year-old mystery, their heroism in the face of danger and their thoughtfulness in the way they conducted themselves when Anne Robertson was finally put to rest. Finally, the head of the town council presented Casey and Lexie with gold medallions to commemorate the occasion and to thank the two of them for righting a wrong that existed for so many years. They had, together, rewritten the history of the town.

Casey's sister, Kathy, gave Lexie a big hug, then grabbed Lexie's and Casey's hand. She raised them in the air so that the audience could see. Over thunderous applause she yelled into Lexie's ear.

"What are you going to do on your next date?"

About the Author

John Prophet holds a master's degree in Special Education from Boston University. His professional experience in the field of education covers a wide range of age groups in a variety of settings. He taught sixth graders in public school,taught emotionally disturbed children in a private psyciatric clinic, was a school adjustment counseling in public schools, taught in Headstart classes and taught candidates for the NASD license examination. He served in the military as an Air Navigator in the U.S. Navy and retired as a Commander, having served in the Naval Reserve for seventeen years.

He has created Mystery at Salt Marsh Bridge out of an interest in mystery stories, particularly those that feature the same characters in different siturations, such as Nancy Drew or the Hardy Boys. Casey Miller and Lexie Wentworth will appear again in another mystery.

John is married, has three children and five grandchildren. He is retired and living with his wife, Ellen, on Cape Cod.

Printed in the United States
2089